What did Kincaid expect from her anyway?

An apology? An argument? Kate nervously wound her fingers together.

After another few minutes of uncomfortable silence, Kincaid finally spoke. "Would you like to give me your version of the story, Ms Matthews?"

"What story?"

Much to Kate's astonishment, he smiled.

His teeth were white and even, his lips sensual. As the unexpected smile spread across his face, it lit his eyes and softened his expression. His eyes were hazel, with little flecks of gold in the outside rim.... Incredible eyes.

"Any story you'd like to start with. The episode of my parking spot. The tête-à-tête at the nurses' station during working hours. This letter I found on my desk." He fingered it with his strong surgeon's hands. "Yes, why not start with the letter?"

Kate swallowed, almost too mesmerized by his eyes, his voice, to speak. "The letter..." She had to pause to run her tongue along her dry lower lip. "The letter seemed like a good idea at the time."

Dear Reader:

We hope our December Harlequin Romances bring you many hours of enjoyment this holiday season.

1989 was an exciting year. We published our 3000th Harlequin Romance! And we introduced a new cover design—which we hope you like.

We're wrapping up the year with a terrific selection of satisfying stories, written by your favorite authors, as well as by some very talented newcomers we're introducing to the series. As always, we've got settings guaranteed to take you places—from the English Cotswolds, to New Zealand, to Holland, to some hometown settings in the United States.

So when you need a break from the hustle and bustle of preparing for the holidays, sit back and relax with our heartwarming stories. Stories with laughter . . . a few tears . . . and lots of heart.

And later, when you get a chance, drop us a line with your thoughts and ideas about how we can try to make your enjoyment of Harlequin Romances even better in the years to come.

From our house to yours, Happy Holidays! And may this special season bring you a lasting gift of joy and happiness.

The Editors
Harlequin Romance
225 Duncan Mill Road
Don Mills, Ontario, Canada
M3B 3K9

LETTERS OF LOVE

Judy Kaye

Harlequin Books

TORONTO • NEW YORK • LONDON
AMSTERDAM • PARIS • SYDNEY • HAMBURG
STOCKHOLM • ATHENS • TOKYO • MILAN

ISBN 0-373-03021-5

Harlequin Romance first edition December 1989

Printed in U.S.A.

CHAPTER ONE

Attractive, intelligent, fun-seeking nurse, age 27, seeks correspondence and companionship from professional man in medical field, age 30-40.

"MULGREW, YOU TRICKED ME! You said it was just for fun. I'll never believe *you* again!" Katherine Matthews's complaint swelled through the empty corridor surrounding the fourth-floor nurses' station of Fargo's St. Mike's Hospital.

"Sure you will. You always do." Molly patted Kate's shoulder consolingly.

"This time you've gone too far." Molly Mulgrew had been embroiling Kate in wild schemes since the days they'd roomed together in nursing school, where Molly's knack for "creative entertainment" had cost them more than one tongue-lashing from the dean. Angrily Kate rumpled her blond curls with her fingers. Was there any more damage the irrepressible Molly could do?

"You owe me forty-five dollars."

"What?" Kate shrieked, then glanced contritely down the long white corridor, hoping she hadn't disturbed any patients.

"Forty-five dollars," Molly whispered. "That's what it cost me to place the ad." The murderous look in Kate's eyes made Molly add, "*Now* maybe I've gone too far?"

Kate wondered in dismay how she was ever going to stop her friend from doing these irresponsible half-baked things.

Molly had spent forty-five dollars for an ad in the Personals column of the *Health Care Journal*! What next?

It was a rhetorical question. Kate had three responses to the ad in her pocket right now.

"It's your own fault, you know," Molly chided bravely, her china-blue eyes wide with innocence, her improbable blond hair looking more suited to a models' runway than a hospital corridor.

"*My* fault? *I* didn't talk me into helping you to compose a 'man wanted' ad. You did! *I* didn't type it up and send it to a magazine." Kate poked a finger at Molly. "You did! *And I'm certainly not going to give you forty-five dollars to cover your expenses!*"

"That's not what I meant," Molly hissed. Furtively she glanced down the hallway. No call lights were blinking over the patients' doors.

Kate ran her hands over the crisp white cotton of her uniform, flexing and curling her fingers in frustration. She hated being included in Molly's crazy schemes. They were twenty-seven years old now. Grown-ups. How could Molly have done this to her again?

It had all begun one Saturday evening two months earlier, when Molly had been in an unusually glum mood. "What's wrong with us, Katie?" she moaned. "Here we are, two gorgeous females with no dates on a Saturday night. Why?"

Kate had smiled and continued drying their supper dishes. "Nothing is wrong with us. I'm glad to be home tonight."

"Then what's wrong with *you*, Kate? You're so...domesticated. Content." Molly's tone was disparaging. "Satisfied with your life."

"You make it sound as if those things are bad. I think I have a great life. Men aren't the be-all and end-all, you know."

"Hah!" Molly poured herself a second glass of white wine.

"In fact, I turned down a date with Brad Jurgens to have dinner with you this evening."

"You did what?" Molly catapulted from her chair.

"Don't be so dramatic. I simply prefer your company to Brad's." Brad, a medical-supplies salesman, was dull compared to Molly.

"It would help, Katie, if you weren't so opposed to meeting men in bars," Molly observed, "but maybe you're right. Those aren't the kind of guys for us, anyway. The trouble is the quality of available men. What we're lacking is not only quantity but quality." Molly was pensive as she paged through a stack of magazines Kate had borrowed from the hospital. "Now, where could we find some quality men?"

Suddenly Molly squealed with glee and waved a copy of *Health Care Journal* in the air. "Listen to this, Katie! There's a Personals column in here. 'Slim and single forty-five-year-old woman seeking relationship with fifty-five-year-old doctor...' Can you believe it? People actually write these things!"

"I suppose they do," Kate replied. "Loneliness does odd things to people sometimes."

"Let's try it." Molly headed for the desk. "We can write one as good as these. Better, even!"

"What on earth for?"

"For the fun of it. We're alone and it's Saturday night. Come on, Katie, don't be so serious!"

Kate had finally given in to Molly's overwhelming ebullience, never dreaming that Molly would actually *mail* the ad....

"It *is* your fault, Kate." Molly's defensive whine brought Kate back to the present. "I may be the one who mailed it, but I did it for you."

"And how, might I ask, do you explain that?" Kate stared blankly at the envelopes she'd pulled from her pocket. They were all addressed to KIM, an acronym for the initials of her own name.

"Your love life, of course."

"What love life?"

"My point exactly!" Molly crowed, jabbing a pink-tipped finger at the pocket of Kate's uniform. "You don't have one!"

"I'm very happy with my life, Molly. Don't try to fix something that's not broken." She'd never met a man to whom she was truly attracted, but that was no reason to start scouring the streets for one now.

"You just don't realize that it's broken." Molly studied her friend's picture-perfect features. Kate's blond curls tumbled across her shoulders in abandon, released from the chignon she normally wore beneath her nurse's cap. "Why's a beautiful woman like you sitting home Saturday nights, anyway? You should be out doing the town."

"May I remind you that I work Sundays?" Kate's green eyes flickered with irritation. "You're a professional, Molly. You, of all people, should understand the importance of rest. We care for people's *lives*!"

"A mere technicality," Molly rejoined, accustomed to Kate's disapproval. "If you refuse to go out and seek male companionship, then the least you can do is take a look at the personals." She grinned mischievously. "Think of it as shopping by catalog rather than taking a trip to the department store." Molly stretched out a hand for the envelopes. "Now then, let's read those letters."

Before she could pull the packet from Kate's grasp, the cool unnerving voice of Dr. Chase Kincaid reached them.

"Another work break, Nurse Matthews? Nurse Mulgrew?" From the corner of her eye, Kate could see three call lights blinking in her section of the corridor. "I thought I saw you both in the lounge only half an hour ago."

Kate swallowed uncomfortably. If the new hospital administrator hadn't been angry with her this morning, after that embarrassing little incident in the parking lot, he certainly was now. Kincaid had arrived at St. Mike's less than a month ago and already everyone felt like they were treading on eggshells.

She glanced at him. He wasn't angry; he was furious. It was obvious from the tense lines etched from his nostrils to the corners of his lips and the irritated tic in his left cheek. Kate suddenly realized that in spite of his black look this man was extremely attractive—and she wished she'd inspired an emotion other than anger.

The surprising thought was gone as quickly as it had come. With a sinking sensation at the pit of her stomach, she stumbled over an apology. "This isn't what it seems, Dr. Kincaid. Those call lights just came on. Nurse Mulgrew and I—"

"—were not attending to duty." His voice was crisp. "At the end of your shift please come to my office. I'd like to speak with both of you." Then he swung around on the heel of his Italian-made shoe and walked off. Kate stood transfixed by the wide sweep of his suit-clad shoulders and the confident easy roll of his step. She sank weakly onto the stool behind her.

'Whew!" Molly sighed gustily next to Kate's ear. "That was close."

"Just close? We're in major trouble, Mulgrew!"

This certainly wasn't the first time Molly had overstepped the bounds of good sense, pulling Kate with her. There was the time in nursing school when Molly had signed Kate's name to the petition requesting that men be allowed to spend the night in the students' quarters. And the incident in which Molly had volunteered Kate's time to the Santa Service, and she and Kate had wound up spending the entire weekend before Christmas in Santa suits, handing exploding cigars to participants in a Shriners convention. The list went on. Kate gave her friend a withering glare before darting down the hallway to respond to the call lights.

It was nearly an hour later when the two reconnoitered at the nurses' station. A group of nurses who'd just come on duty stood clustered around the desk. Dropping her charts onto the already teetering stack, Kate slumped onto the nearest stool and cradled her forehead in both hands.

"A run-in with Kincaid, huh? He's been a busy man since he arrived from Chicago," Kitty Frank commiserated. "He's been here a month and already come down hard on just about every employee in this hospital."

"See? I told you it was no big deal, Kate," Molly put in. "As soon as the new head honcho thinks he's scared us all into submission, he'll relax and things will be normal again. You'll see."

"Not necessarily," Kate said grimly. It was mortifying enough to be reprimanded by the hospital administrator, but for some reason the rebuke seemed doubly embarrassing coming from Kincaid.

"Not to worry. Things will be fine," Molly soothed.

Kate's eyes felt tired and scratchy. This had been a long and difficult day, with one problem after another, culminating in the scene with Kincaid. Oddly, having to confront him now made her feel like crying. "You've only had one run-in with him today," she pointed out. "This is my second. My car ran out of gas this morning and I coasted into the parking lot—and stalled right behind his parking space. He had to park in the visitor lot until the tow truck came. He wasn't too cordial, even after I explained."

"The man has Freon in his veins. He's chilly as an air-conditioning unit," Kitty volunteered as she made notations on a chart.

"Yeah," someone else added. "If they did an autopsy on him, they'd find nothing but granite inside. He's already laid off a fourth of the custodial staff."

"What?" Kate gasped. Surely the board wasn't laying people off again!

"You should hang out in the coffee room more often, Kate. You're behind on the latest gossip. The scuttlebutt is that the hospital board brought Kincaid in to tighten things up around here," Molly told her. "He was running some fancy private hospital in Chicago for the past two years, but wanted to get back to actually practicing medicine. I suppose they figured that since he's a doctor, as well as an administrator, he could see patients in between doing his hatchet jobs."

"Let's hope they're small cuts," John Hanson, one of St. Mike's male nurses, commented. "We can't afford to lose any more staff."

Kate felt a wave of dismay. They *were* shorthanded. On some floors there simply wasn't enough help to prepare the patients for morning rounds or to deal with more than a single emergency at a time. She and Molly hadn't helped matters by arguing over the ad when there was work to be done. Kate didn't want to be responsible for convincing Kincaid that Floor Four had too many nurses—or worse, inattentive ones.

The rest of Kate's shift dragged interminably. Yet it wasn't really the day's events or even the reprimand from Kincaid that distressed her. It was fear of his reaction to the list of requests she'd delivered to his private secretary early that morning.

Kate was the elected spokesperson for the nurses at St. Mike's, a great honor, as well as a show of trust by her peers. For the past month she had basked in the glory of her election. Now it seemed the work had begun.

There had been several recent clashes between St. Mike's nurses and physicians. The nurses maintained that since they were the primary care givers during a patient's stay in the hospital, they should have a greater voice in patient care. Most of the physicians were unwilling to give up any shred of authority unless they were forced by the administration.

Kate had prepared a letter to Kincaid asking that he implement changes in the hospital's policy toward nurses; she also asked that he restructure nurses' responsibilities and raise their salaries accordingly. This important plea lay on Kincaid's desk right now, its impact no doubt blunted by the fact that it was written by a nurse he obviously considered frivolous, if not downright incompetent.

That ill-timed gab session with Molly might have ruined her chances of ever convincing Kincaid how crucial it was to recognize the professional and emotional needs of the nurses at St. Mike's. Instead, she'd probably convinced him that two of the nurses on Floor Four weren't tending to business.

Molly, looking serene and composed, glided up behind her. "Shift's over. Are you ready?"

"Aren't you worried?" Kate asked.

"Me? Worried? About Dr. Gorgeous-but-Grumpy Kincaid?" Molly waved a hand in the air. "Nah. He just wants to scare the bejeebers out of everyone during his first month here so he can earn a little respect." Her eyes sparkled with confidence. "I'm a good nurse, and if he's looked at the records, he knows it."

Though Molly was probably right, it didn't make the trek to the administrative offices on the main floor any more pleasant. The antiseptic tiled halls seemed longer than usual, the sounds more hushed and ominous. Kate cast a panicked eye along the corridor to where Kincaid stood waiting in the door of his office.

Kate's stomach turned fluttery as he lifted one of his well-shaped eyebrows. The speculative expression in his eyes made her legs feel weak, but despite her nervousness, she had to admire his startling good looks.

"Ms Mulgrew, Ms Matthews, I've been expecting you." Though his voice was pleasantly rich and deep, Kate could sense his barely contained irritation. The two trailed after him into the outer office.

"Have a seat, Ms Matthews." Kincaid gestured toward a pair of intimidatingly formal wing-backed chairs. "I'd like to talk to Ms Mulgrew alone for a moment. Then I'll have a word with you."

Kate watched Molly's rigid white back disappear into the inner office, then sank into one of the leather chairs. It was even more uncomfortable than it looked. Like waiting in a school principal's office, the whole situation was humiliating—and entirely of her own, and Molly's, making.

Kincaid's secretary was already gone for the day, and Kate found the silence nerve-racking. To calm herself, she glanced through the magazines on the table. A familiar journal caught her eye and she reached over to flip it open. There it was in bold black and white.

> Attractive, intelligent, fun-seeking nurse, age 27, seeks correspondence and companionship from professional man in medical field, age 30-40. Write KIM, c/o Health Care Journal, Box 809...

Molly had thought of everything, she mused. It had been an especially clever move to take Kate's initials—Katherine Ingrid Matthews—and create an acronym to protect her privacy. Kate sighed deeply. She supposed she should at least be grateful that her identity was still a secret.

Kate dropped the magazine as Molly came hurtling through the office door. She was flushed a bright unhealthy pink under the peroxide blond of her hair. Kate's eyes widened as Molly grimaced. If Kincaid had dented Molly's devil-may-care attitude, he could roll over *her* like a bulldozer over a tin can.

"Ms Matthews, could you step into my office?" He stared at her with an unreadable expression in his hazel-colored eyes, and unexpectedly Kate shivered. Taking a deep breath, she resolutely followed him inside.

She was vaguely conscious of the rough tweedy texture of his suit and the heady masculine scent he wore. More than ever, she felt like a small child summoned to the principal's office for a reprimand. Still, no child would be so conscious of the easy graceful manner in which the man walked or the contained strength of the well-formed body beneath the suit...

The office had been redecorated, Kate noticed, forcing her mind from the delicious tour it was conducting over Kincaid's physique. Row after row of thick medical volumes lined the walls. The gleaming mahogany paneling was the room's only ornamentation.

"Have a chair."

Kate complied and nervously wound her fingers together.

Just when she thought the silence would suffocate her, Kincaid spoke. "Would you like to give me your version of the story?"

"What story?"

Much to Kate's astonishment, he smiled.

His teeth were white and even, his lips sensual. As the smile broke across his face, she noticed his eyes—hazel, the entire spectrum of chameleonlike shades that the human eye can be. Brownish-grayish-bluish green. And his had little flecks of gold in the outside rim. Incredible eyes.

"Any story you'd like to start with. The episode in my parking spot. The tête-à-tête at the nurses' station during working hours. The letter I found on my desk." He fingered it with his strong surgeon's hands. "I'm willing to begin wherever you wish."

Kate swallowed. This...amicability was almost worse than his anger.

"Ms Matthews?"

Kate felt mesmerized by his eyes, his voice. The adrenalin seemed to be pumping through her system at record speed, and her mouth was so dry she didn't trust herself to speak. When she finally found her voice, it was thin and reedy. "I'm sorry if you thought Molly and I were shirking our duties this afternoon. The calls lights *had* just come on. We weren't ignoring them—no matter how it appeared to you. And—" she swallowed the bowling ball lodged in her throat, "—just because Molly and I were, uh, visiting, it doesn't mean you've got too many nurses on the shift."

"Did I say that I did?" He dropped his gaze to the file on his desk.

"No, but I've heard—"

He looked up. The shaft of light behind his eyes had disappeared, and they were suddenly as hard and colorless as granite. "Yes, Ms Matthews, tell me what you've heard."

Kate groaned inwardly. She hadn't meant it to come out like that. She didn't want to repeat hospital rumors to Kincaid.

"Nothing definite, I'm afraid," she parried. "Just the usual questions that arise when a new administrator takes over...."

"So you won't say? Is that it?"

She had the grace to look away. With that combination of sternness and compelling masculinity, Kincaid flustered her more thoroughly than anyone she'd ever met.

"Ms Matthews?" He was waiting for a reply.

"Rumors, sir. Nothing more. It's natural that staff would wonder about policy changes."

"Or personnel cuts?"

Kate felt as though she'd been punched in the stomach. "Or personnel cuts."

He took a pair of glasses from the top drawer of his desk and sat tapping the ear pieces together thoughtfully. Finally he slid the glasses onto the bridge of his nose.

They should have made him less handsome. Instead they made him more so. He looked intelligent, wise and oddly enough, kind. He truly matched the austere bookish room about him.

"Would you like to talk about the letter I received from you concerning the nurses' requests?"

"It's fairly straightforward, I believe. I laid things out as clearly as I could. I was elected by the nurses as their spokesperson. The nurses want more responsibility for decisions concerning patients and more input into hospital functions." She paused to run her tongue across her dry lower lip. "The letter seemed like a good idea, what with the change in hospital administration and all."

"And what would you like me to do, Ms Matthews? Give the nurses full run of things and a pay raise as well? Would you be able to explain that to the physicians and the hospital board?"

She bit the soft inner flesh of her cheek. He was baiting her, but she wouldn't let him trip her up. The requests in the letter were valid. "I believe you're exaggerating my position, Dr. Kincaid. We just want a little more responsibility and authority where our patients are concerned."

"Above that of the patient's physician?" Here was the real bone of contention.

"Nurses are responsible for a patient twenty-four hours a day, sir. The doctors are with them for a few moments during rounds. It seems the primary care giver should have the right to make some decisions about a patient's well-being.'' Kate lifted her chin defiantly as she spoke.

Then, just as she was readying herself for a verbal battle, he inquired, ''Did you get gas for your car?''

Kate blinked. ''What?''

''Gas. For your car. Isn't that the excuse you had for blocking my parking space today?''

She wondered why Kincaid seemed bent on provoking her. What did he expect from her, anyway? An apology? An argument?

''The filling station called. It was the fuel pump, not an empty tank. They towed it away.''

''I see.'' Kincaid acted as though he did see something Kate couldn't fathom. And somehow that made her strangely uncomfortable.

Apparently he wanted to play mental games, but he'd have to find another partner. ''If our meeting's over, I think I should be going, Dr. Kincaid,'' she said abruptly. ''I'd like to catch a ride home with Molly.''

''I should think Ms Mulgrew's halfway home by now. I'm afraid I frightened her.'' He sounded more amused than regretful.

''Frightened Molly? That takes quite a bit of doing.'' Kate remembered her friend's quick departure and suppressed a grin. Actually Molly deserved a good scare after what she'd done to Kate.

Kincaid's lips curled into a smile that didn't quite reach his eyes. ''I gather that all of this hospital's employees believe their heads are on the chopping block—and picture me with the ax in my hand.''

''Is that so?'' Kate ventured. The tiny smile had made him seem more approachable.

''Perhaps.'' His eyes darkened. ''I'm not sure of my strategies yet. The board has some high expectations.''

''And whatever they ask you'll do?''

"It's my job. St. Mike's is suffering a severe monetary slump. I was hired to put it back on track." He shrugged resignedly. "I'll do what's necessary."

Kate was startled by his intensity. There was a hidden agenda here somewhere, she sensed, something that made Kincaid care deeply whether or not St. Mike's sank or swam. Whatever it was, he didn't seem likely to divulge it to her.

"Did you leave a private practice behind in Chicago?" she asked politely.

He slipped off the glasses and Kate felt a pang of regret.

"Yes, a very small one—I was running a private hospital. I'm planning to have a larger practice here at St. Mike's, in addition to my administrative duties."

"Won't that be very demanding and time-consuming?"

"I have plenty of time." Time, his tone indicated, he had in abundance, though he obviously didn't intend to explain why he had so little outside of his work to occupy it.

"Well, Ms Katherine Matthews, I'll take your letter under consideration if, that is, you'll promise to limit your in-depth conversations with Ms Mulgrew to the lunchroom."

"Agreed."

Kincaid nodded crisply. Realizing she'd been dismissed, Kate self-consciously made her way to the door. At the threshold, his voice stopped her. "Need a ride?"

She whirled around. "Sir?"

"A ride. Your car is in the shop. Do you need a ride home?"

"I...uh...well, if Molly's gone...I can call a cab and..." Much to her dismay, she was stammering like a schoolgirl. The idea of riding somewhere—anywhere—in close quarters with Dr. Chase Kincaid made her feel breathless and awkwardly adolescent.

"No problem. I'll drop you off. I have the time."

It was no less a command than any of the others he'd given her today. Since refusing a ride seemed tantamount to insubordination, Kate followed him toward the parking lot.

He spoke little except to inquire about her address as he pulled the gleaming New Yorker into rush-hour traffic. Kate settled wearily against the velvety fabric seats, enjoying the air-conditioned coolness that washed across her face. The day had been a difficult one, and she was grateful Kincaid didn't seem to require conversation.

"Is this it?" he asked a few minutes later, breaking the silence that had fallen between them. Kate smiled as the familiar view of home came into sight, and nodded. Once a grand old house, it was now divided into three apartments. She occupied the top floor, an apartment with slanted ceilings, huge windows and unpredictable plumbing.

"It's very quaint," he remarked.

"The old-fashioned charm and coziness were what first attracted me." She smiled ruefully. "Too cozy in the summer sometimes, so I've recently installed an air conditioner."

"Nice neighborhood?"

"Very. Mostly families. All the houses are well kept and there's a junior high nearby, where the—"

"A school?"

He sounded sharply attentive and Kate looked at him in surprise. "Are you house hunting?"

"Sort of."

"And you want to be near a school?" The rumor mill hadn't said anything about Kincaid's being married.

"Maybe." His voice was suddenly remote. But then he smiled apologetically and his next words were friendlier. "It hasn't been decided yet whether my children will be coming to Fargo or not. If they do, I'd like to be near a school."

Divorced. Maybe that was why he had so much extra time.

She rested her palm against the door handle. "Well, thank you for the ride, Dr. Kincaid."

Somehow she expected him to say, "Call me Chase," but he didn't. Instead he nodded curtly, dismissing her as effectively as he had in his office. An unexpected wave of disappointment engulfed her.

"No mixing business and pleasure," she muttered to herself as she watched the big silver car roll away. Probably a good thing, though, she mused. There would no doubt be some very unpleasant business between them before this nurses' rights-and-responsibilities thing was resolved.

Inexplicably saddened by the thought, Kate sighed and strolled up the stairs to the topmost gables of the old house.

CHAPTER TWO

"WHAT DID THEY SAY? Huh? Huh? What'd they say?" Molly's head popped around the doorjamb like a sideways jack-in-the-box.

The dish Kate was holding clattered to the floor. "You startled me! Don't you ever knock?"

"I knock at the bottom of that long staircase and you never hear me. Then I knock on the banister all the way up. Then I peek into the apartment and you drop something and ask me why I don't knock. It happens every time." Before Kate could respond, Molly added, "Well, what did they say?"

"Who?" Kate snapped, as she bent to retrieve the dish. Molly was getting on her nerves. First the hospital, now this.

"The letters, of course!"

"Oh, those. I almost forgot!" Kate had taken a quick nap, clothes and all, after Kincaid had left. Reading the letters hadn't even occurred to her.

"How could you forget something so important?" Molly yelped. She scanned Kate's counter for something to eat and settled on a carrot stick.

"It was your ad, not mine. Anyway, I had lots on my mind. After Dr. Kincaid dropped me off, I—"

"Kincaid dropped you off!" Molly squealed. "He tells *me* to tend to business, scares me half out of my wits and then offers to take *you* home! Why, that—"

"Don't get excited," Kate warned as she picked up the bowl of raw vegetables and carried it to the kitchen table.

"My car is in the garage being repaired. You'd already left. I suppose he thought it was the polite thing to do."

"So, what's he like away from the hospital? Does he shed that haughty reserve like a soiled lab coat? Is he warm? Is he wonderful? Is he...?" Molly waved her arms theatrically, the carrot stick bobbing like a director's baton.

"He's exactly the same as he is at the hospital."

"Oh." Molly's arms dropped to her sides. "I was afraid of that. Delightful to look at, prickly to touch."

Kate grinned. "Right. But you didn't come all the way over to hear about Kincaid, did you?"

She was relieved when Molly took the bait and changed the subject. "The letters! Let's see the letters!" Together they settled at Kate's kitchen table and began to read.

Molly could barely contain herself. "Listen to this, Kate—this man is from Wisconsin. A hospital pharmacist. Divorced with three children. He's interested in meeting a woman in the medical profession. Says his marriage broke up because his wife didn't understand his commitment to medicine." Molly leaned back in her chair, a dreamy faraway look forming in her blue eyes.

"I'll bet," Kate retorted. "More likely he's a workaholic who didn't come home at night." Sometimes Molly was so naive about men.

Still shaking her head, Kate stared thoughtfully at the letter in front of her. Typed on expensive vellum, it smelled faintly... woodsy. Like men's cologne.

"Then how does this one sound?" Molly asked, after scanning the third letter. "It's from a male nurse. Age thirty-four. Single. Wants to correspond with a woman in the same profession. Hmmm..." She became very quiet.

"What else?"

"Oh, nothing." Molly's voice was vague. "He just sent a picture." Kate peered over her friend's shoulder. Molly was obviously impressed by the swarthy handsomeness of the man in the photo.

Kate grinned. "If you like him, you can have him."

"Huh?"

"You mailed the ad. So you write to him. He's not my type."

Molly rested her elbows on the table, studying her friend. "And just what *is* your type, anyway?"

Kate shrugged. "Haven't found him yet."

"Obviously." Molly's expression turned pensive. "What's the man of your dreams like, Kate? Try to describe him."

"Tall, dark and handsome," Kate retorted. "How's that?"

"Not good enough. How tall, how dark and how handsome?"

"Six foot two, not very dark, and *very* handsome."

"Like Dr. Chase Kincaid?" Molly's look was sly.

Kate gave her an irate glance. "I wouldn't know. I didn't notice if he was any of those things."

"Hah!"

Molly returned to the letter she was reading and Kate pretended to do the same. But the image of Dr. Kincaid's face—in that brief moment when he'd smiled at her—remained.

"How's yours?" Molly asked.

"My what?" Kate was still lost in her memory of Kincaid.

"Your letter, silly! What's it like?"

Kate stared at the page. "Odd, really. A mix of sophisticated and childishly charming." As Molly came closer, Kate found herself holding the pages protectively to her chest. "He's a doctor."

"A doctor. Ohh! That's good! So doctors get lonely, too. That's nice to know." Molly sniffed the air and added, "Scented, too!"

"I know. That's part of what's sweet. It doesn't seem to be from the type of man who would splash cologne on his stationery."

"What does it say?"

"He's a doctor with a young family. Divorced, from the sound of it. The rest of the letter is just as though he's writing to an old friend. He talks about a patient he's treated, a wonderful vintage wine he's discovered, and then—" confusion creased Kate's brow "—suddenly it says, 'All for now. Please answer my letter.' The return address is Chicago."

"Are you going to?"

"Answer the letter? Of course not. I didn't mean for anyone to write to me."

"But they did. And they're each expecting a reply."

"You reply. You started this."

"You helped compose the ad. I remember."

"Too much white wine and giggles composed that ad. We were acting like schoolgirls." Kate paused. "But I suppose we should write and tell them that KIM isn't interested in corresponding."

"It's only the polite thing to do." Molly agreed triumphantly. "You take the doctor. I'll break the news to the pharmacist and the nurse."

"And," Kate insisted, "any more of these things that filter in." It was only fitting that Molly take responsibility for the letters—she'd started all this nonsense. Besides, Kate suspected from the dreamy expression on Molly's face, that good-looking male nurse wasn't going to get a rejection letter, anyway.

Eagerly, Molly scooped the two letters into her pocket. "Gotta go. I've got things to do."

"Letters to write, you mean," Kate muttered as she saw her friend to the door. After Molly left, Kate curled up cozily on the couch with a cup of tea. Thoughtfully, she reread the scented letter.

"Dear Miss Kim," the black type began. "I've never answered an ad before, but I wanted to answer yours."

The letter continued, "You interested me because you are a nurse and you're from the Midwest. I'm a doctor. I have two children. I am divorced."

Then abruptly, as Kate had previously noticed, the letter switched tones. It became informal and chatty, speaking to her as though she were an old friend. The paragraphs glowed with a warmth and intelligence she found intriguing. And just as abruptly, the relaxed informal style ended with: "All for now. Please answer my letter." It was signed with the initials C.G.

At the bottom of the page, was an urgently underlined postscript: "Please write to C.G. at Box 809...."

Carefully, Kate tucked the letter into its envelope. *Please write.*

Why would a doctor, obviously successful and intelligent, want to answer an ad in a Personals column? She stared unblinking out the window at the lush oak branches brushing the eaves and rustling in the wind. The soft sibilant murmur, like old-fashioned crinoline petticoats, was a lonesome, restless sound.

Lonesome. Was that what Doctor C.G. from Chicago was?

And how about Kate Matthews? Was she lonesome, too?

Yes, Kate admitted to herself as she stripped off her uniform and stepped into the shower, sometimes she was. This treetop apartment, as she liked to call it, could be too quiet, especially after growing up with five brothers and sisters in a three-bedroom home. For years, Kate had wanted nothing more than a place of her own—peace, quiet and first chance at the bathroom. But lately...

Minutes later she shook off the thought with the waterfall of drops from her hair. That was *still* all she wanted.

She glanced into the steam-fogged mirror and caught a hazy glimpse of her curving outline as she moved about the bathroom. She didn't need anyone else, she reminded herself. Especially not a man. The large dark smudges that were her eyes stared back unbelievingly.

Kate was roughly toweling her skin when Melvin sauntered through the bathroom door. He stood poised in the doorway and stared at her with accusing blue eyes.

"Hi, Mel. Did you miss me today?"

"Meowwww." The answer was a strung-out wail.

"Hungry?"

He gave her the disdainful look only pampered pets can give, and Kate returned a contented smile. This was as crowded as she needed to be. One demanding male was enough for any woman.

The phone rang just as Kate finished serving Melvin his gourmet kitty chow. She wrinkled her nose as she wiped her fishy smelling hands on the front of her terry robe before picking up the phone. "Hello."

"Kate! This is Marlis Owens."

"Hi, Marlis. What's up?" Marlis was the supervisor of student nurses. Kate often teased her about being as patient as Job and calm as the Sphinx, necessary qualities for marshaling the students through their stint at the hospital. Tonight she sounded upset.

"It's Dr. Nash. That man has tormented me and my students for the last time! It's going to be either him or me, Kate. I simply won't tolerate any more of it!"

"Whoa, Marlis. Slow down. What's Nash done now?" Dr. Nash was short-tempered, impatient and demanding—a notoriously difficult doctor to work with.

Marlis's voice trembled with suppressed fury. "He called one of my students names I wouldn't call rats in a cellar. He simply cannot treat the nurses with this callous lack of esteem any longer."

"He treats everyone the same, Marlis. You know that." A heaviness settled in Kate's stomach. If Marlis and Nash were going to butt heads, she'd be caught right in the middle.

"I want you to file a formal complaint with the hospital administrator, Kate. You're our representative. You take care of the details and I'll sign anything I need to. Nash has got to be put in his place."

"But Marlis—"

"No *if*s, *and*s or *but*s. I'm serious, Kate."

"Then I'd better talk to Dr. Kincaid," Kate offered unhappily. A face-off with him was something she'd prefer to avoid. Especially after today.

"What's Kincaid like, anyway?" Marlis asked curiously, already calmer now that she'd spoken her piece.

"Intimidating. Efficient. That's about all I've observed." Kate didn't mention his piercing, multicolored eyes or the sensuous fullness of his lower lip.

"Handsome. That's what *I've* observed," Marlis said craftily. "Lucky you. You get to sit down across from him at the negotiating table. Nice view."

"Lucky me," Kate sighed after she hung up the phone.

Melvin did a series of figure eights between her ankles until she picked him up and settled him on her lap. Her eyes fell to the envelope on the coffee table. The letter.

She reached for the pad and felt-tipped pen on the corner of the couch. The writer deserved a reply. Just a short one. A simple "thanks but no thanks" would do. Or would it?

She considered the conversational style of the body of the letter. At least she could tell the author a bit about herself.

He deserved that much. Then she could guiltlessly explain that she wasn't interested in corresponding. Her first attempts, however, seemed stilted and dull. It wasn't until she reread the letter that an idea came to mind. She would read a line or two of C.G.'s letter and then respond as though she were talking to him.

Kate rubbed her eyes in astonishment when she'd finished the three-page letter and glanced at the clock. It was after midnight. Writing her reply had turned out to be much easier than she'd expected— rather fun, really. Too bad this was going to be their only correspondence.

At the bottom of the final page she'd written, "I hope you'll find someone else with whom to exchange letters. I think it's better to end our correspondence while we're only initials and post-office-box numbers to one another. Thank you for taking the time, best wishes in your career, and goodbye."

Unaccountably she felt just a bit sad that she would never know C.G. of Chicago.

The next morning arrived too early. Kate groaned as the alarm shrieked its unwelcome call, but as she rolled to turn it off, she tossed her full weight across Melvin who was sleeping next to her. He meowed a complaint and scurried out from beneath her, scratching her arms in the process. Kate groaned again as she scrambled out of bed to find the antiseptic lotion and tend to her wounds. Melvin watched her from the edge of the bathtub.

All the way to the hospital, Kate held a debate with Chase Kincaid, imagining him in the seat next to her. She sharpened her wits and refined her arguments about the foul-mouthed and generally unpleasant Dr. Nash. By the time she reached the parking lot, her case was prepared.

As she walked toward the administrative offices, she regretted accepting the position of spokesperson for the nursing staff. At the time, she hadn't counted on Chase

Kincaid—or the disquieting effect he had on her. She couldn't predict her own emotions around him, let alone guess what his responses might be.

Kincaid was in the hallway outside his office, talking to an elderly woman in a wheelchair. Rather than have the trembling gray head incline to look up at him, he'd hunkered down next to the big spoked wheel of her chair. His hand lay comfortingly across her forearm and his eyes were riveted on the woman's lined face.

Kate could see the amber flecks in his eyes dancing with pleasure as he spoke to the old woman. Although the hall crackled with activity, he took no notice of anyone else.

Kate felt a strange burst of envy. She couldn't remember the last time someone had looked at *her* with such obvious interest and concern. The gentle smile he gave his gray-haired friend made him as appealingly youthful as a first-year med student. The nervous knot in her stomach softened. Kincaid was human after all.

The conversation drew to a close as Kate neared, and Kincaid unfolded himself from his squatting position. A woman in a blue smock glided out of the admissions office to steer the elderly woman's wheelchair toward the bank of elevators. Kate could see a gentle smile lift the corners of Dr. Kincaid's mouth.

His expression hardened as he turned toward the bustling hall, and as his eyes met Kate's the harsh lines that so often marked his features returned and his shoulders stiffened. She could almost see his reserve, like a thick curtain, shuddering into place. Kate envied the old lady even more.

"Good morning, Ms Matthews. Are you looking for me?" He tucked his hand into the pocket of his trousers and angled his lean muscular body toward the wall.

"Yes, do you have time to talk?"

He nodded toward his office, inviting her inside.

She could feel the warmth of his body and smell the delicious fragrance of his cologne as she passed him. It was an oddly familiar sensation. Before she could question why, he handed her a cup of coffee, his long fingers strong and sure around the ceramic mug. She saw that his nails were clipped and meticulously clean. Kate liked his hands. They looked gentle, skillful, sensitive—all the qualities she liked in a physician. And in a man.

"Coffee?" His voice prodded her to attention, and Kate nodded dumbly. Once again, Kincaid was making her feel like an infatuated, giddy schoolgirl. She declined cream and sugar as she took the mug he offered and wrapped her hands around it. Raising it to her lips, Kate inhaled deeply of the coffee's dark rich aroma.

Impulsively she asked, "Have you begun seeing your own patients yet?"

"You mean the lady in the wheelchair?"

"Maybe. You seemed so attentive I just thought . . ." She let the words fade away but he didn't seem to find the questions intrusive.

"Not yet. I just happen to have a fondness for gray hair and wrinkles."

Kate's eyes must have asked what her lips didn't, because Kincaid chuckled. "You haven't heard, then? My specialty is geriatrics. I don't consider anyone a prime candidate for my practice unless their sixtieth birthday is only a memory."

"Oh." Kate regarded Kincaid with new respect. It took a very special sort to deal with the aged.

"I started out to be a pediatrician," Kincaid explained as he gestured her to a chair and slid into his own behind the massive oak desk. He folded his tapering fingers across the white expanse of his shirt, resting them on his stomach. "It's not such a jump from pediatrics to geriatrics as it might appear."

Kate was intrigued. He seemed softer and less intimidating today, talking about his profession. She observed him with a sudden unexpected rush of admiration. Kincaid's eyes focused somewhere over the top of her head, his mind captivated by thoughts at which she could only guess. He straightened suddenly and plowed his fingers through his hair. "Sorry, I didn't mean to drift away like that. You must have had a purpose in looking me up so early this morning." The smile lines around his eyes deepened.

It was miraculous, really, Kate decided. While Dr. Kincaid was lost in his thoughts—whatever they were—the tension left his face and took a dozen years with it. In those moments he looked youthful, approachable and startlingly handsome.

Kate regretted her own mission. Kincaid wouldn't stay mellow for long once she began her story. She drew a deep breath and plunged in, speaking quickly. "I had a call last evening from the supervisor of student nurses. She wants me to file a complaint with you."

"Concerning what?" Wariness invaded his expression.

"One of the doctors has been verbally mistreating some of the student nurses."

Kincaid's eyes flashed. "There are things that nurses have to get used to, Ms Matthews. Doctors flaring up under pressure is one of them."

Kate's own temper flared up. "And do they have to get used to the same doctor patting their behinds when he thinks no one else is looking?"

She hadn't meant to say that; the words had just slipped out. Nash's lecherous behavior wasn't the basis of Marlis's complaint, but it was common hospital knowledge. Kate had talked to enough nurses who were afraid to file a complaint to know it was true.

"What?" Kincaid was leaning forward on the desk, white-knuckled and angry.

"I'm sorry. I shouldn't have mentioned that. The complaint I've been asked to file concerns only a name-calling incident."

"But you did say it, Ms Matthews."

She regretted the fact more with each passing moment.

"And who is this Romeo we're discussing?"

"Dr. Ardon Nash."

"Nash?" Kincaid's eyebrows arched. "He's one of the most adept surgeons on staff. His credentials are impeccable."

"The nurses aren't questioning his credentials, sir."

"You're venturing into an area strewn with land mines, Ms Matthews. *That's* what you're doing."

"I'm sorry, but Nash has had a reputation for his quick tongue and even quicker fingers for a long time. Long before you came to this hospital."

"And you and the other nurses have chosen this particular time to discredit him?"

"Dr. Kincaid!" That wasn't the point of her complaint at all, but Kincaid obviously chose to interpret it that way.

"I'll look into this alleged verbal harassment, Ms Matthews. There's a procedure to be followed in cases like these. Naturally I will follow it to the letter. You can assure your colleague that if her charge is verified, it will be dealt with accordingly."

"Are you implying that I, as spokesperson for the nurses, would come in here if I didn't believe this complaint was legitimate?" Kate was breathless with anger.

"Surely a man as well educated as Nash would have enough sense not to—"

Kincaid was applying his own sensibilities to Nash. A grave mistake, Kate thought to herself. He'd better get his idealistic head out of the clouds soon if he expected to be an effective administrator!

"Since when do men have the monopoly on good sense?" she demanded.

"It seems to me that you're overreacting, Ms Matthews. If you want your judgment and position as spokesperson respected you should—"

"And it seems to me, Dr. Kincaid, that you're reluctant to do your job as administrator of this hospital! When a nurse who has been on staff for fifteen years calls me with a complaint such as this one, I have to believe her."

"You can't believe everything you hear, you know. If I called a physician up on the carpet every time a nurse complained about something he or she did, I'd be left with—"

"Competent employees who respect one another," she retorted. "You've inherited a staff of very fine nurses, Dr. Kincaid. If you plan to keep them, I suggest that you take their complaints seriously. Dr. Nash was out of line."

"You have your views and I have mine," he replied coldly, his eyes narrowed in displeasure. "Though it's difficult to believe that Dr. Nash would do anything so foolish, I'll look into it. And," he added, "for my own information, I'll also look into your little off-the-record allegation about Nash's roving hands." He rose from his desk in a brisk signal of dismissal. "That will be all for now, Ms Matthews. Thank you for coming. Good day."

He ushered Kate to the hallway where she stood bewildered, irate, affronted. "So he thinks I'm overreacting!" Her knees quivered and her face burned a hot, furious pink. She hadn't asked him to give Nash his walking papers, for heaven's sake! Is that what he'd thought she wanted? The man could turn from genial to frigid in the blink of an eye. She glanced at the wall clock and sighed. Only eight-thirty. The day had barely begun.

Already Kate knew that she never wanted another confrontation with Kincaid. He obviously saved his kind affectionate moments for his elderly patients. The staff seemed destined to know only his alter ego, the cynical man who had just made Kate's insides churn with emotion.

By the time she reached the Floor Four nurses' station, she felt as though someone had set a bonfire in her cheeks. As the day progressed her irritation didn't diminish, and a flicker of anger arose within her each time the name of Dr. Chase Kincaid was mentioned.

CHAPTER THREE

KINCAID WAS AS GOOD as his word.

Via the hospital grapevine, a communication mechanism that Ma Bell couldn't rival, Kate learned that several student nurses and their supervisor had been called to Kincaid's office. Word was out that Dr. Nash had also been summoned to the administrative office for an evaluative procedure of some sort. She knew full well the true reason, although the grapevine was strangely quiet on that count.

Kincaid's quick silent action helped to neutralize Kate's antagonism. He was a true professional. And after all, Kate rationalized, she didn't have to *like* the man to work for him. Perhaps now she could go about her business as before, she concluded with satisfaction.

But that was not to be. Much to her dismay, just as things were returning to normal, Kate received another complaint, and she was forced to gird herself for another showdown with Kincaid.

Brushing a weary hand across her eyes as she updated charts at the nurses' station, she recalled the conversation she'd had with Mary Edwards.

Mary, a steady competent professional whom Kate would have entrusted with her life, had come to her deeply troubled.

"We need to talk, Kate." Mary's plain kindly face was lined with worry. Distractedly, she pulled at a hank of mouse-brown hair that had escaped from beneath her nurse's cap.

"Sure. Lunchtime okay?"

"Now." The undisguised tension in Mary's voice brought Kate's head up with a jerk.

"Mary? What's wrong?" Concerned, Kate studied the woman's face.

"Let's go someplace private." The emphasis was on private.

"Sure. The supply room?" It almost seemed a silly place to suggest, Kate thought, but it was also the most truly private place in the hospital. There was a reason that those old jokes about interns and nurses carrying on romances in hospital supply rooms still existed. The more logical place to talk, the coffee room, seemed equipped with an invisible loudspeaker to the rest of the hospital. Anything discussed there was common knowledge within hours.

"Fine." Mary's normally soft voice was ragged. She led the way, her white-soled feet rushing silently across the tiles.

Once they were ensconced in the tiny airless cubicle, surrounded by bedding and cardboard boxes of supplies, Kate asked her gently, "What's this all about?"

"I think I've got a problem, Kate. I have a patient who's rapidly becoming very weak and disoriented. He's going downhill so quickly, I..." Mary bit nervously at her lower lip.

"Have you talked to his physician about this, Mary? Perhaps he can..."

"That's the problem, Kate. I have. More than once. I believe the disorientation is drug-induced. My patient's doctor doesn't agree with me. I'm sure the medication I'm administering is doing more harm than good." Mary grimaced. "He told me that when I finished medical school to come back and we'd talk about it."

Kate felt a rush of indignation. It wasn't the first time a member of the nursing staff had been subjected to such comments—herself included.

"I think the patient should have another doctor check him. Another opinion," Mary said. "Dr. Kincaid's opinion."

"Do you know what you're asking?"

"I'm asking you, as our spokesperson, to go to Kincaid. Tell him what I've told you. I've written down what I think is important for him to know. Give this to him, and ask him to look in on the patient."

"Perhaps you should do this yourself, Mary. Kincaid and I..." How could she say that already she and Kincaid weren't seeing eye to eye?

"I think you should do it," Mary insisted. "I want to go through the proper channels. Then I'll answer any questions he might have for me."

"It's not Dr. Nash, I hope?" Kate muttered gloomily. That would be the final straw.

Mary gave her an uncomprehending look. "No, it's not Nash. But please, Kate, talk to Kincaid. And soon."

Half an hour later Mary's plea still echoed in Kate's ears. "Whoever told me I'd be good in politics must have thought I was a masochist," she muttered.

"What was that?" Molly inquired, stepping up behind Kate's stool.

"Masochist. Masochist. That's what a person has to be to act as liaison between the nurses in this hospital and Kincaid." Kate threw her pen across her clipboard and pressed the heels of her hands against the aching spots in her temples.

"Is he that bad? I've been hearing good things about what he's been doing with some of the departments. Gerontology, especially. And the head anesthetist, Dr. Annie Martin, has nothing but praise for him."

Kate blew a strand of golden hair away from her face with a gusty breath. "Not *bad*, really. Just, well, difficult." Kate thought back to the episode over Dr. Nash and to the little run-ins she and Kincaid had had since his arrival.

She slumped on her stool, sighing heavily. She didn't want to think about Kincaid right now. He was like a pebble in her shoe, a distracting, nettlesome irritant. What she needed was a complete diversion, something to get her mind off the building tension at the hospital.

At the end of her shift, Kate left the hospital stealthily, not wanting to be cornered by Molly and her inevitable hundred questions. Kincaid's car was still in its parking space. No matter what shift she worked, he seemed to be at the hospital. It was maddening. She couldn't even grouse about his errant work habits.

Kate shook off her discouraging thoughts as she entered the foyer of her apartment house. She needed something—anything—to get her mind off work.

Her wish was granted with the afternoon mail. Despite all her protestations about not corresponding with the mysterious C.G., Kate's weariness and depression lifted as she spied the letter atop the other mail in her box.

The envelope was of the same rich vellum as the last. The neat type spelled out her acronym—KIM. Suddenly she realized he'd sent this letter to her home address. How had he found it? Then she remembered. The Christmas gift from her mother—stationery with a return address faintly embossed on the envelopes!

Kate smiled wryly. She certainly hadn't thought of everything. Her hands were trembling as she turned the letter over and over in her fingers. She hadn't wanted this to happen...had she? She'd wanted C.G. to understand the finality of her message.

She was tempted to toss the long ivory envelope into the trash and to pretend she hadn't received it. That might be the wisest course. After all, she'd sent him a reply, explaining that she didn't care to correspond. Why hadn't he taken her seriously? And yet...

Her hand hovered over the waste basket. She suspended the letter daintily between forefinger and thumb, ready to drop it. Abruptly she pulled it back, consumed with curiosity. She would read it first, *then* throw it away. What the letter said made no difference, she reasoned, but at least her curiosity would be satisfied.

Methodically she poured herself some lemonade, arranged the perspiring glass on a coaster and took it to the couch. Once she was settled in the soft pillowed corner, she carefully slit open the letter with a fingernail.

Slowly, with a precision she usually reserved for the operating room, Kate lifted the smooth paper from its enclosure. She studied its faintly scalloped top edge before her eyes traveled to the typewritten words below:

Dear Kim,
I know you asked me not to write again, but I had to. I think that we could become good friends if you'd only give me a chance.

I've thought of you often these past days, wondering how you are and what you're doing. I imagine you rising in the morning, your cheeks rosy with sleep and your hair tumbled about in wonderful abandon....

Kate's eyes grew round with amazement. The letter was exquisitely composed—sensitive, tender...loving. A courtship on paper. She felt a blush rising in her cheeks. How dare a stranger address such intimate words to her?

Her gaze fell again to the letter and her anger was momentarily melted away by the gentle, melodic phrases. She dropped the paper onto her lap and stared out the window into the tops of the trees.

C.G. was quite a romantic at the typewriter. Kate had known a number of doctors in her time, but she'd never imagined one of them wooing a woman in such a lyrical manner. As much as she wanted to deny it, her curiosity was piqued.

As she turned to read the letter again, she heard a commotion on the stairs, then Molly popped through the doorway carrying an array of white cartons from the Chinese carry-out downtown. "Egg-roll time! Hot mustard, sweet-and-sour spare ribs, and Lok Ping's special chow mein to top it off. Sound good?"

"Wonderful! But what inspired this?" Kate jumped up to spread the cartons across the coffee table.

"It's a celebration." Molly opened the first carton and popped a morsel of sweet-and-sour pork into her mouth.

"And what are we celebrating?" Discreetly, Kate tucked the letter behind a pillow on the couch.

"Remember the letters we got through the ad?"

"How could I forget?" Kate didn't attempt to keep the sarcasm from her voice.

"I decided since you wouldn't write to those guys, I would." Molly grinned a Cheshire cat grin. "And I got replies from both of them today!"

"The mails must be busy," Kate commented wryly.

"They both sound terrific." Molly poked at the pillows on the couch, arranging a nest in which to sit. "I think you made a big mistake not—What's this?" Molly plucked the envelope from its hiding place.

Kate flopped back against the sofa with a sigh of resignation. "I got a reply of my own."

"You did answer it, then! Good girl! I knew if I sent that ad in your name you'd—"

"I wrote and told him I didn't want to write to him again. But he wouldn't take *no* for an answer." Kate nodded toward the envelope. "In fact, he seems to have interpreted *no* as a green light."

Blatantly curious, Molly turned the open flap toward the floor and shook out the paper. Two pieces of paper drifted to the floor.

"What's this?" Kate sprang for the small square card she hadn't noticed in her earlier reading.

It was a photograph, a Polaroid shot, badly composed. The subject was partially obscured, his face and left shoulder blocked by the shadow of a large sail. Muddy and incomplete though the photo was, Kate found it intriguing. She could see little of the subject's face, but his body, naked to the waist, wet and gleaming, was an anatomical study of perfected muscles.

"That's one gorgeous bod!" Molly observed over Kate's left shoulder. "Too bad the face is in shadow."

"It's an odd picture to send, don't you think?" Kate mused, more curious than she cared to admit about the face that might accompany that body.

"I think it's...titillating." Molly studied the photo speculatively. "I want to meet the man who lives in that set of muscles. Don't you?"

Do I? Kate stared at the photo. Things were getting out of hand. Now she was beginning to imagine the mysterious C.G. as a human being—with a rather spectacular physique at that. He was no longer a bodiless entity.

The image stayed with her all through supper. Through Molly's chatter and noisy departure. Through her shower. And through her dreams.

MARLIS OWENS FOUND Kate in the lunchroom. The red mottled splotches on Marlis's neck immediately told Kate that something important had gone awry.

"What's wrong, Marlis? You look like you're ready to explode."

"Wrong? You'd be better off asking what's right. That would only take a second to answer." She flung herself into the chair across from Kate's and muttered, "We've got troubles."

"We do?" Kate echoed. "Now what?"

"Dr. Nash. I'd like to chop that man off at the knees. Or higher, where it would do some good."

"This sounds serious."

"Whatever Kincaid told him about my complaint has only made him angry. Now he's mad at me—and you. Furious, actually. And he's found a nasty little way to get even."

"What?"

"He's on a vengeance campaign. He's been rereading all the incident reports for the past year. I think he's hoping to find our names on enough of them to point it out to Kincaid."

An incident report was filed each time something occurred in the hospital that shouldn't have. If a patient fell out of bed or wandered away from his room, a report was filed. If a patient was mismedicated or injured, it was written up. Too many incident reports on one's record was something every nurse wanted to avoid.

"Terrific," Kate groaned, ardently wishing that she could be *un*elected staff spokesperson. "And who's going to take care of his patients while he's playing detective?"

Marlis missed Kate's bleak attempt at humor entirely. "He's out to get us, Kate. If not with the incident reports, then with something else. We're going to have to be on our toes from now on. We've made Nash mad. Any slip ups and he'll have Kincaid crashing down on us."

"I don't plan on making any slip ups, Marlis. Just be sure not to take any verbal orders from the doctors. That's really the only place you could inadvertantly make an error. We're good nurses. Don't forget that."

"I only wish Dr. Kincaid could see Nash for what he really is: a small-minded, vindictive—"

"Dr. Kincaid took care of your first complaint, didn't he?" Kate pointed out.

"Yes. Very professionally. And quietly, thank goodness."

"Well, give him a chance, then. Maybe he'll be able to see through Nash, now that he's confronted him once." Kate listened to herself in amazement. Here she was, defending Kincaid, the man who could incite her to anger more quickly than anyone else she'd ever met.

Another showdown was almost inevitable. Kincaid was so absolutely correct in his behavior, so professional, that he probably had difficulty imagining one of his peers behaving in any other manner. Unfortunately it might be her job to convince him that someone could stoop to petty or even unethical conduct.

"I have to see Kincaid about another matter. I'll talk to him about the incident reports if the opportunity arises, Marlis. And by the way—" she stood up and looked down at her friend "—if someone talks me into running for this post again in the next election, don't vote for me."

HIS DOOR WAS AJAR. Kate took a deep breath and rapped on the elaborate oak portal.

"Come in."

As always, she was startled by his rugged handsomeness. His coat was tossed carelessly across his desk. He'd loosened his tie and it rested, rakishly askew, near his collar. He wore a crumpled shirt with the sleeves rolled up and was gluing the wing on a large toy airplane.

"I'm sorry. I didn't realize you were still in surgery."

He glanced up at Kate's words and grinned, his eyes a kaleidoscope of color. "It's all right. This patient will live."

"I didn't know you collected model airplanes."

"Not just model airplanes, *radio-controlled* model airplanes. There's a big difference. Anyway, it's my son's, not mine. I just promised to have it fixed by the time he arrived."

"Your children are coming?" The prospect made Kate curious. What kind of children would Kincaid have fathered? Handsome ones, no doubt.

"Yes. Nathan is a precocious thirteen going on forty-five, and Emily is eleven going on twenty," he said in a manner that was half-proud, half-awed. "They've grown up so quickly."

"Tell me about them." Already Kate guessed their eyes to be hazel with flecks of amber.

Kincaid smiled. Clearly, Kate had touched a subject dear to his heart. "Nathan's my problem solver. I think he'll be a diplomat someday, or a politician. He's always seeing what he calls *situations* and trying to remedy them." Chase grinned and leaned back easily in his chair. "Sometimes he only creates *more* trouble with his interference. Just ask his sister."

"Emily? What's she like?"

"So far Emily's more interested in causing problems than solving them. Nathan can talk her into anything, and then he blames her when whatever they've done goes sour. She's terminally curious, too. Someday that's going to be her downfall. Anyway, I've decided to buy a house and they'll be arriving here this weekend to help me choose it."

He paused, and Kate waited quietly for him to continue.

"My wife and I share custody," he explained in a flat, emotionless voice. "She has the children during the school year, and I have them summers, holidays and as many weekends as possible. I want the children to feel comfortable here, so it's probably best they help choose a house." Kincaid shrugged. "I really don't care where I live."

So things weren't all perfect in Kincaid's life. Kate felt herself warming to him, felt moved and oddly gratified by his unexpected confidences. Instead of asking the questions that immediately came to her mind, she murmured. "I'd like to hear more about them. About Nathan and Emily."

Kincaid's rugged features creased into a smile. "Nathan is a take-charge sort of kid. He's very bright—takes a lot of advanced-level science and math. He's a mediator. He wants everyone to be happy all the time." Kincaid's eyes darkened and their beautiful flecks of amber dimmed. "Our divorce was very hard on Nathan. He didn't want to see his parents unhappy. Now that my ex-wife has remarried, he's eased up on her, but he still worries about me."

"What does he worry about?"

"That I won't take time to eat when I'm at the hospital, that I'll drive too fast, sleep too little. That I'll be lonely."

"Sounds like a heavy burden for a thirteen-year-old."

Kincaid nodded. "I'm glad Emily has a different personality. She's easygoing, carefree. And she adores her older brother. She'd do anything for him."

"Lucky him."

"Maybe. But one day he'll get both of them into some sort of mischief that they can't get out of without my help. Still, I'm looking forward to having them with me. I've missed them." An edge of loneliness crept into Kincaid's voice, and against her better judgment, Kate felt herself softening toward him even more.

"Any ideas where you'll settle?"

"There's some possibility that the kids will be staying with me for longer periods of time, so I want to be near a good school. That's the primary concern. There are some nice homes available in your neighborhood, I hear."

Kate experienced a jolt of alarm and stared down at her hands to conceal it. Kincaid in her neighborhood? Was that a good idea? Especially considering the intense but unwilling attraction she felt toward him. She didn't need her life any more complicated by Kincaid than it already was. Chatting pleasantly with Kincaid at the hospital was one thing; it was quite another to have the man himself living nearby. That seemed too much like bringing one's work home from the office.

Before she could pursue the thought he inquired briskly, "So. What can I do for you, Ms Matthews?"

While she looked away, he'd managed to roll down his shirt sleeves and straighten his tie. She wished he'd left them alone. He'd appeared more approachable before.

She spoke before her nerve left her. "I've had another complaint, sir." Her tongue tangled several times as she poured out Mary's story concerning the wrongly medicated patient. When she was through, Kate held her breath.

"I'll look into it."

Was that all? No deprecating remarks? No disagreement? "Sir?"

"I said I'd look into it. I don't like nurses second-guessing physicians, but I do realize that a nurse spends more time with a patient than the doctor does. I'll check it out personally."

Kate felt a surge of relief. She'd worried for nothing. That heady sense of relief made her plunge headlong into the other bit of information still plaguing her. "There's something else."

Kincaid, who had already turned his attention to a chart, glanced up. "Yes?"

"I'm afraid we're going to have to discuss Dr. Nash again."

Kincaid's pleasant demeanor vanished. "Nash? I believe that's been taken care of, Ms Matthews."

"I'm afraid not. Marlis Owens says he's very angry with her and with me."

"Is that so?"

Was his tone cooler than before? Kate wavered a moment but forged ahead. "He's checking the incident reports from the past year. She believes that he's, uh, out to get us."

"Hardly professional behavior." Kincaid's jaw tensed, which only emphasized his strong masculine profile.

"I agree, sir, but Dr. Nash has been known to—"

"I mean on Nurse Owens's part."

"Sir?" Kate's jaw dropped in amazement.

"She's reported an irregularity and now she expects revenge. I find that highly unlikely. Dr. Nash has been very cordial. Perhaps Nurse Owens should extend the same courtesy toward Nash."

If Kincaid had dropped a grenade at her feet, she couldn't have been more surprised. "Dr. Kincaid! Marlis is not a small-minded or vindictive woman! She has reason to believe that Nash will attempt to cause trouble because of the report—"

His eyes darkened and his voice was taut with anger. "What we're discussing here is pure speculation. Not every woman is as noble as you assume, Ms Matthews. I've had more than a little experience with that."

Kate's eyebrows arched in surprise. Through her own anger, she wondered what his peculiar statement meant. "Because you've had a bad experience with one woman, you think all women are troublemakers?" she demanded.

"I'm simply implying that all women are not equally noble or high-minded. Perhaps you should consider that before bringing any more speculative complaints about our best surgeons."

Kate's mouth worked, but her fury wouldn't allow any more words to emerge. Was he defending Nash? Or demeaning women in general?

Before she could find her voice, he continued, "I'll keep this new accusation in mind, Ms Matthews, just in case I do encounter any problems with the incident reports. But—" he skewered her with his gaze "—please, *please*, caution the people who come to you in the future to be careful about voicing unjustified complaints."

He looked at her, his gaze steely. "If there's nothing else, you may go."

Kate stumbled backward through the door, stunned. How dared he suggest that Marlis was the troublemaker when it was Nash who'd—How could he believe she would come to him if she didn't think what Marlis had suggested was at least possible? How would he—Her mind spun with the implications of their conversation.

She was still fuming when she arrived home that evening. She prowled the empty apartment, desperately needing someone to talk to.

Molly wasn't home. Neither were Marlis nor any of the others she called on the telephone. There was nowhere to vent the blinding rage she felt toward Chase Kincaid.

She paced the floor in a vain attempt to diffuse her frustration. On her third tour around the room, her eyes fell on her most recent letter from the mysterious C.G. It had arrived, despite her continued insistence that she didn't care to correspond.

She picked it up and skimmed the now familiar lines:

> There's nothing finer, more valuable, more precious than knowledge. And with knowledge comes understanding. That's something we don't treasure enough these days, I'm afraid. Tolerance, the willingness to understand, would alone strengthen interpersonal relationships tenfold.
>
> But I'm rambling again. Just finished a nineteenth-century novel by an obscure writer. Makes me

philosophical and I'm taking it out on you...

C.G.'s letters baffled her. They were such an odd combination of astute intelligence and naïveté, tender words and philosophical digressions. They were like a patchwork quilt, bits of wisdom, snippets of childishness, fragments of affection, all sewn together.

Impulsively she carried the letter to the small rolltop desk in the corner of the living room. He valued understanding, did he? Well, that must mean he was an understanding man. Perhaps she could express to this faceless, nameless correspondent of hers the anger she was feeling toward Dr. Chase Kincaid....

He's churlish, unreasonable and suspicious most of the time. He doesn't seem to take people seriously unless they're physicians with as many initials after their names as he has after his, or they're white-haired and pushing eighty.

He's a very frustrating man, C.G.—volatile, unpredictable, difficult to understand. What makes a man act that way? Perhaps he's unhappy in his private life, but he shouldn't take it out on the nursing staff of our hospital....

Her pen flew across the pages, picking up momentum as her anger and frustration erupted—first about Nash and his sly, offensive ways, then about the more important issues, the inequalities that the hospital and its board and administration seemed so bent on preserving. And, ultimately, about loneliness.

She'd never really felt lonely before, Kate thought. Not in twenty-seven years had she felt anything but self-sufficient, self-sustaining, whole. But during the past few weeks she'd changed. Perhaps Molly was right after all. Perhaps she needed someone special in her life more than she'd realized. She resolutely pushed away the image that came fleetingly to mind—the warmly smiling eyes of a man talking with love and concern about his children.

Melvin wrapped himself around her ankles as she sat staring through the window into the treetops. His purr amplified when she lifted him onto her lap. Kate murmured a question into the soft beige fur at the nape of his neck. "But who, Melvin? Who do I need?"

His answer was to knead his needlelike claws on her skirt and put more volume into the rumbling purr. She chuckled. "Are you telling me that all I need is you, Mel?"

But deep inside, she sensed a growing realization that she needed something—or someone—more.

KATE GLANCED BACK at the blue-and-white mailbox with trepidation. It was done. The letter was mailed and on its way to Chicago. But this letter was different from the earlier ones. This time she'd signed her name.

It had seemed like a good idea last night—to explain that KIM was an acronym for Katherine Ingrid Matthews. It still hadn't seemed such a bad idea this morning. But now that there was no turning back, now that the letter was firmly in the jaws of the mailbox, Kate was beginning to doubt her decision.

Due to a serious bus accident and the resulting busy emergency department, there was no time for reflection on the letter that day or the two following. By late afternoon of the third day, Kate was eager to leave work and return to the solitude of her treetop apartment.

Bone weary and aching with exhaustion, she decided to melt away some of her tension by sunbathing in the yard. Armed with a woven mat, a small towel and a large bottle of suntan lotion, she settled herself by the side of the house, as much out of view from the street as she could manage.

This was the only time she regretted the dense back-yard trees with their light-blocking canopy of leaves, which precluded any private sunbathing.

She lay half-asleep, oiled and unmoving, floating in that never-never land between wakefulness and somnolence that sun worshipers relish. Only the occasional barking of a dog or the conversation of passersby reminded her that she wasn't alone on her very own sun-warmed planet.

"I like this house!"

"Yeah! It's great. Look at all those little peaks at the roof. This looks like a mansion!"

Kate opened one eye. It was her house they were talking about, she was sure. Whoever *they* were.

Two children, almost teens. She could see them from the corner of her eye. The boy was long and lanky, his size already hinting at the tall handsome man he would become. He wore faded denim jeans and a fashionably crumpled cotton shirt. The girl was petite and trim, dressed in brief black shorts and a black-and-hot-pink T-shirt with a panda logo on the front. She exuded vivaciousness and good humor.

Good-looking kids, Kate thought drowsily. She closed her eyes. Maybe they'd go away.

"Can we look at this house? I'd like to live here."

"This house is already taken, I'm afraid."

Kate's mental eyes flew open, though she managed, with much difficulty, to keep her lids squeezed shut. That voice was extremely familiar. The voice moved closer.

"In fact, one of the nurses at the hospital lives here."

"She does? Do you think she could show us around?" The girl gasped in delight. "I'd love to see how it looks inside."

"I don't know. Why don't you ask her?" A soft chuckle followed. "She's lying right there."

Kate grimaced inwardly. Caught sunbathing. By Dr. Chase Kincaid. In the skimpiest scrap of a bathing suit she owned. She opened her eyes to find Kincaid's hazel ones staring down at her. From her position on the grass he was upside down. It didn't harm his good looks one bit.

"Hello."

"Dr. Kincaid."

He carefully avoided looking at her bikini top, glancing instead toward the roof gables of the building. "My children have been admiring your house."

Kate struggled to her feet, all the while trying to keep her full breasts inside the scant top. She'd known her figure was too lush for this style when she'd purchased the suit, but until now, she'd always sunbathed alone.

She felt virtually undressed, and by the look in the teenage boy's eyes, she might have been. At least his father, because of his years as a physician, had cultivated a more impersonal gaze.

She jerked the towel about her waist, wishing she had another to wrap around her shoulders. But wishing didn't make one appear. If she fell out of the bikini top, she fell out. There was nothing more she could do.

"Did I hear some people say they wanted to look around?" she asked.

"Yeah!" was the chorus.

The girl's eyes were dark and bright with excitement. "This is the most wonderful house I've ever seen!"

"Then follow the brick path around to the back to see the rest of the yard. When you've done that, come upstairs to the top floor and I'll show you my apartment."

The pair beat a path around the corner of the house, leaving Kate and Chase to stare at one another. His eyes darted in every direction but that of the tiny scraps of fabric Kate wore.

Chase cleared his throat. "Well."

"Deep hole with water in it." Kate grinned, finally regaining her composure. "Want to come upstairs and sit on my couch while I put on some clothes? Perhaps you could pour some lemonade for the kids while I'm changing."

As soon as she'd said it, she wondered if she'd been too forward, but her fears were quickly stilled.

He smiled widely. "Love to. And you definitely need more clothes. My son will have eyestrain if you walk around in that handkerchief and two bandages you call a bathing suit." The flecks of gold in his startling eyes gleamed.

His medical education hadn't trained *all* the life out of him, then, Kate thought with perverse satisfaction as she led the way upstairs.

"Nice place." His voice was very near her ear. Goose bumps rose along her bare skin, and a feather of nerves teased her insides.

Covertly Kate watched him amble through the tiny apartment. The sloped roof, which gave the place its charm, kept him at the center of the room, where his head didn't touch the angled ceilings. With his large, masculine presence, the apartment fairly screamed of Kate's dainty meticulous femininity.

"Here, make yourself useful." Kate handed him a sweating pitcher of lemonade, her voice ragged with breathlessness. She was eager to change into less-revealing clothes.

Kate left him pouring lemonade into tall plastic tumblers while she slipped into hot-pink shorts and a vibrant teal blouse. She pulled her hair away from her face with pink and teal combs and whisked some lip gloss across her lips. When she returned to the living room, Chase and the two children were seated at the round kitchen table.

"This is like living in a tree house!" the little girl bubbled. Her brother nodded in silent agreement.

"How long have you lived here?" the boy finally asked.

"Nearly five years." Kate smiled. It was hard to believe she'd worked at St. Mike's that long.

"Do you know if anybody downstairs is planning to move out?" the boy asked hopefully. He had eyes like his father's—intelligent and compelling. Kate suppressed a grin. He was going to be a head turner in the not-too-distant future, no doubt breaking more than one teenage heart.

"House hunting, I presume," Kate commented as she poured herself a glass of lemonade.

"Very astute. So far nothing but this place has attracted any interest. And I hadn't really planned to buy an apartment house."

"Well, maybe Miss...Miss..." The girl paused nodding toward Kate. "Maybe she knows of some other houses like this one!"

Chase laughed. "Maybe. But I see that I've been remiss. I didn't introduce you properly. Kate, these are my children, Nathan and Emily. They've come from Chicago to help me find a house. Children, this is Nurse Katherine Matthews."

Emily smiled widely at Kate, showing a mouthful of gleaming braces. Only a doctor could afford such an array of metal, Kate thought.

Absently she turned to glance at Nathan Kincaid, and her eyes widened in alarm. The boy seemed to be ill. All the color had drained from his face and his features were pinched and sharp. He was staring at her, with a strange dismayed expression on his face.

"Nathan, are you all right?" Chase had noticed his son's change of appearance, too.

"Do you need to lie down?" Kate jumped up from the table to lay a finger on the boy's pulse.

"No, I...I just feel funny all of a sudden. Like I'm going to throw up." His voice was faraway and tinny, as though he were whispering through a long metal tube.

"Three tacos and fried ice cream for lunch," the doctor diagnosed. "I'd better get you back to my apartment before Kate ends up working overtime."

Chase propped the boy up under the armpits and supported him with an arm across his shoulders. "Okay, son?" Nathan stood there limply, casting doleful glances toward Kate.

She followed the three on their halting procession downstairs. "I hope you feel better soon, Nathan," she consoled.

He nodded weakly. Blotches of feverish color in his pasty white face made him appear even unhealthier. Kate wondered what could have caused such a rapid transformation. It was almost as if... but it couldn't be! It was almost as if the boy were *afraid*.

When Chase had deposited him gently in the back seat of the car, Nathan's eyes darted from his father to Kate and back again. He sat up on his elbows as if he wanted to speak, then dropped back against the velvety cushion without uttering a sound.

"I'd offer to help you with him, but you're the doctor," Kate said.

"Thanks. But sometimes we aren't so good with our own families." Chase smiled grimly and threw a worried glance toward the back of the car. "I'll call you if I lose perspective."

Thoughtfully Kate watched the vehicle pull away. As it turned the corner, she saw Nathan's head poke up over the top of the seat and peer back at her as she stood in the driveway. She wondered again what had happened to the boy to make him change so quickly. Was he really ill? Or was there something else in those hazel eyes, so like his father's? Could it be what she'd first thought it was?

But why would the boy suddenly be ill with fear?

CHAPTER FOUR

KATE WHISTLED CHEERFULLY as she made her way down the checkered tile hallways of St. Mike's.

"Aren't you chipper this morning," Molly grumbled, passing Kate in the hall. "Whistling? Before breakfast?"

"I had breakfast two hours ago," Kate replied pleasantly. "Eggs, toast, juice, black coffee..."

"Ugh." Molly didn't come truly alive until noon or later.

"Don't be a grump, Mulgrew. I even rode my bike to work."

"That old clunker?" Molly was as determined to be grouchy as Kate was to be cheerful.

Kate only smiled. It was a beautiful day. The sun was shining, the birds were singing, Chase's car was already in the parking lot....

An even wider smile tickled the corners of her lips. Since when did the sight of Kincaid's car put her in such a wonderfully giddy mood? she wondered.

Since last night—since she'd seen him in the role of a normal human being, a father. A man who was warm and relaxed, who traded quips and—Just then, the subject of her whimsy stepped into her line of vision.

"Good morning, Ms Matthews."

"Hello." Kate couldn't keep the breathless pleasure from her voice. "It's a marvelous sunny day, isn't it?"

"Yes, I suppose so."

Kate tipped her head to one side and stared into the amber-flecked eyes. "You suppose so?"

Kincaid smiled apologetically. "I was at work before the sun came up."

"How's Nathan? Was he ill last night when you got him home?"

Kincaid shook his head. "Funny, but he seemed to settle down after we left. He didn't have a fever or stomachache, and he insisted he was fine until I finally had to believe him." Kincaid shrugged in bemusement. "If it were one of my patients, I'd say he'd had a stress attack or something equally vague. Maybe Nathan's still suffering from the trauma of my divorce. You can't discount these things." His concerned frown made him appear suddenly vulnerable.

"But he slept well last night?" Kate asked, refusing to be drawn into speculations concerning such private matters.

"In fits and turns. I could hear him babbling in his sleep. He quieted down toward morning." Kincaid ran his long lean fingers through his hair, leaving a rumpled trail through the thick strands. "I'm still worried about him, though. Who knows with a kid his age? Illness, hormones, peer pressure..."

"Perhaps he's just growing up, Dr. Kincaid. It happens, you know."

"But not to *my* children!" he protested in an amused voice. "That means I'm getting old."

He didn't look the least bit old, Kate decided as she studied the broad, square sweep of his shoulders and the bronzed line of his jaw. He looked perfect to her.

Suddenly Kincaid seemed to realize that he was dallying in the hall, making small talk with a nurse on duty. "I'm keeping you from your work, Ms Matthews. I'm sorry."

I'm not.

Aloud, Kate murmured, "You have nice children, sir. I'm glad Nathan's all right."

Kincaid nodded brusquely, but the hint of a smile pulled at the corners of his mouth.

As they parted and Kate moved toward the nurses' station on Floor Four, her disposition was decidedly better than it had been earlier that morning—which hardly seemed possible.

Her mood was eroded, however, by a day full of minor complaints, cross and irritable patients and a broken air-conditioning system.

"This day is lasting forever," Molly whined as she tapped her pen on the stack of charts on the desk.

Kate nodded. It already seemed like days since she'd run into Chase in the hallway and had that pleasant, slightly furtive conversation. "We're almost off duty," she announced, glancing at her watch. "I'm going to run some information down to the main office right now, before I leave for the day."

"Ta-ta," Molly trilled. "If you see Kincaid, blow him a kiss from me."

Kate didn't bother responding to Molly's outrageous statement. Instead she gathered up the bundle of papers she'd been sorting and headed toward admissions.

Her step was so brisk and her mind so preoccupied that Kate almost missed seeing Nathan Kincaid sitting forlornly outside his father's office.

"Nathan! Hello! How are you feeling today?" Kate asked, pausing by the boy's chair. Nathan slouched awkwardly in the stiff-backed seat, shoulders rounded, chin low on his chest, looking dejected.

"Okay."

"Are you waiting for your dad?"

"Yeah."

"Where's your sister?" Kate suddenly wished she'd never started this uneasy, one-sided conversation.

"Outside."

He looked and sounded so miserable that Kate bent down, lightly resting her hand on his shoulder. "Does your dad know you're here?"

When the boy shook his head, Kate asked, "Are you sick? Would you like to have him paged?"

"His secretary said he was in conference. I didn't want to interrupt him so I said I'd just wait. Emily wanted to stay outside. She doesn't like the smell of hospitals."

"I don't blame her," Kate agreed. "Fresh air is much nicer."

Nathan raised his head to stare at her. He had the same disconcerting gaze as his father, and she felt as though she were being subjected to a series of X rays.

"Nathan?" she ventured. The boy dropped his gaze and stared instead at the buttons on the front of his pale blue cotton shirt. "Listen, if there's anything I can do for you, anything at all, just let me know."

At his anguished look, Kate hurried on, "And remember, Nathan, you can always talk to your father if you're having problems. I know he's very worried about you."

"He is?" Nathan asked doubtfully. "Do you really think so?"

"I know so. He said you didn't sleep very well last night."

"I just couldn't quit thinking about—" Nathan abruptly clamped his mouth shut.

She perched on the edge of the chair next to his. "I really do think you'd better tell your father what's on your mind," Kate went on. "Whatever it is, I'm sure he'll understand."

"I don't know about that," Nathan muttered. "You don't know what I have to tell him." He gave her a look so filled with distress that it tore at Kate's heart. "He's gonna be mad. Really mad."

What could be worrying this boy so? What haunted teenagers these days? Drugs? It didn't seem likely. Not with

Chase around to notice the first signs of abuse. Peer pressure? That was more probable. School difficulties of some sort, Kate suspected. But he needed to talk out this secret he was harboring, this bit of deep, dark information he was concealing.

"Nathan?" She took his cold, limp hand in her own.

"I don't think my dad's gonna understand at all," the boy repeated. "He's gonna blow his stack but good if I tell him."

"There's nothing a child shouldn't be able to tell his father," Kate said. "Your dad is deeply concerned about your welfare. Whatever it is that's bothering you, whatever you're afraid of, talk it over with him."

Nathan brightened. "You really think Dad would want me to talk about . . . it?"

Kate recalled the look of loving concern in Chase's eyes. "I'm sure he would."

"Well, I'll think about it," the boy said in a doubtful voice. "If *you* think it's okay, that is." He glanced at her hopefully, as if her answer really mattered.

She wondered why her permission was so important to the boy. "Of course I think it's okay," she answered promptly. "I'd feel bad if you made any other decision."

Her reply seemed to settle him. When she left his side a moment later, Nathan was skimming through one of the worn magazines from the rack near his chair. Kate shook her head. What an odd scene that had been. She still didn't know what she and Nathan had been talking about.

The next morning, as Kate began examining the notes left by the night nurses, she was surprised to see a new nurse coming on duty.

"Lissa, what are you doing here? Don't they need you on third?"

Lissa Adamson shrugged. "Must not. I had a message to come up here and take over for you."

"For me?" Kate was astounded. "But why?"

"I don't know. The head nurse said Dr. Kincaid left orders that you were to go to his office immediately and that I was to take over for you until you got back."

Whatever could Kincaid want that was so important? Kate wondered. Was it Nathan? A cold chill wrapped its way around her heart. Had Nathan heeded her advice? Was the child in more serious trouble than she'd imagined? But why would Chase call *her*?

"You'd better get going," Lissa admonished. "From the sound of my supervisor, he wanted you down there in a hurry."

"Will Nurse Katherine Matthews report to the administrator's office immediately." The loudspeaker had flickered to life. "Will Nurse Katherine Matthews report to the administrator's office *immediately.*" Kate's eyes flew to the speaker on the wall. It was rarely used to page nurses—only doctors, or to announce a Code Blue—an emergency.

Kate, more than a little curious about the imperious summons, gave Lissa a pat on the shoulder. "Thanks for helping out. I'll be back as soon as I can."

The tiled hallway seemed endless as Kate hurried toward the elevators. What could possibly be wrong? Perhaps it was a personal matter—a death? By the time she reached Kincaid's office, Kate had conjured up every tragedy known to mankind, all of them centered on her family.

Or maybe it's another complaint about Dr. Nash, she thought, twisting the knob on the door to Kincaid's outer office. *Maybe he's finally gone off the deep end and attacked someone.*

Whatever the problem, Miss Oberon, Kincaid's virtually unflappable secretary, did nothing to soothe Kate's nerves. "There you are! Finally! Where have you been? Dr. Kincaid has been waiting for you all morning!"

"The new shift just began, Oberon. I've been on duty less than five minutes."

"Whatever." Miss Oberon's hands dangled loosely from her wrists. "All I know is that Dr. Kincaid wants to see you very badly."

"Well, I'm here now," Kate soothed. It wasn't as though someone were going into cardiac arrest on his office floor! Perhaps everyone was simply overreacting...

The inner-office door flew open and Kincaid burst into the doorway. One look at the fury on his face told Kate immediately that no one had overreacted. Until that moment, she'd always thought the phrase *blazing eyes* was nothing more than a silly cliché for anger. Now she knew better.

"Inside." The word was a clipped command and Kate quickly obeyed.

Kincaid closed the door behind him, then strode to the desk. Silently he picked up a small bundle of paper from the corner and began to slap it against his thigh.

Kate watched from beneath lowered lids. She could see that he was struggling to retain his composure. She felt a bead of nervous perspiration trickle aimlessly down her back. What was infuriating him so? What could be...? Her gaze fell to the packet he was slapping against his leg and she gasped.

Her letters! Chase Kincaid was standing before her, his face contorted with fury, his shoulders rigid with controlled anger, and her letters to C.G. in his hand!

"How did you get those?" she demanded. "They're mine!"

"And apparently they're also mine."

"Yours? But—" Suddenly, the impact of what he was saying avalanched upon her. "I think there must be some mistake," she murmured lamely. She'd mailed those letters to Chicago. How had Kincaid found them?

"I'd hoped that was true," he growled, "but your name *is* Katherine Ingrid Matthews, is it not?"

Kate nodded weakly.

"Surely there can't be another Katherine Ingrid Matthews working at this hospital?"

"No." Her voice sounded small and faraway as she remembered the dreadful things she'd said about Kincaid in that last letter. Things had somehow gone terribly, terribly wrong.

"And I doubt that anyone from this hospital has been using your name without your permission."

She thought of Molly. A weak "not exactly" followed.

"Then I think that you and I are pen pals, Ms Matthews. Not very cordial ones, either."

"But how...? I don't understand..." This was beyond comprehension. How had her letters to C.G. ended up here, in Kincaid's hands? She drew a deep breath and squared her shoulders in a show of bravery she was far from feeling. "You'll have to explain, sir."

Kincaid stopped pacing. He leaned wearily against the top of his desk and stared at a point just above Kate's head. "This is rather difficult."

Some of Kate's shattered poise was returning. "I would imagine." It was good to see that Kincaid seemed no less shaken than she was.

"It's Nathan," he began.

"He's ill?" Kate was quick to inquire, her own crisis momentarily forgotten.

Kincaid laughed humorlessly. "No. Not yet. Not unless I scared him to death."

This conversation had the unreal quality of events in the *Alice* books. Had she stepped through Kincaid's door and somehow fallen through the looking glass? "What about Nathan?"

"He's been writing to you. Letters. To a post-office-box number he found in a magazine."

"*Nathan* has been writing those letters?" How could a child his age have composed those tender and intimate thoughts? It didn't make sense. None of this did.

Kincaid rose to walk around his desk and sank into the leather chair behind it. In a tired voice he told her, "You might as well sit down, Ms Matthews. We have a lot to discuss."

She dropped heavily into the chair, almost inarticulate with shock. Nathan wrote those letters? "But... I don't understand! How...?"

"My son, the problem solver, apparently took it upon himself to ensure that I wouldn't be lonely in my new home. I tried to conceal how wretched I felt after the divorce, but obviously I didn't succeed." His words came softly now. "I didn't mean for the children to know."

And that wasn't meant for her to hear, either, she realized—any more than she was meant to see the flash of sudden anguish on his face. It occurred to her that her mouth was gaping, but she had no will to close it. She stared at Kincaid as he continued.

"When he discovered an ad in the Personals column under Midwest in the *Health Care Journal*, he decided to write." Kincaid paused and laced his fingers together over the papers on his desk. His beautiful eyes were stony agates. "Imagine his delight when he discovered that the response came from Fargo, North Dakota."

Kate's mouth worked but no words came.

"He decided that if I was going to start a new life here—" one of Chase's eyebrows tilted in mock humor "—then he would make sure I had at least one lady friend in the area to count on. So, he pursued the correspondence with 'Kim.' He did it all for me, he says."

"But I still don't quite—" Kate began.

Chase cut her short. "That's why he was so upset at your home the other evening. Nathan's a city boy. He had no idea how much smaller Fargo was than Chicago or that it had so many fewer hospitals. It was quite a shock for him to discover that you already worked for me, since he hadn't yet built up the nerve to tell me what he'd done."

Chase's mouth was a grim line and the cords in his neck tensed even further. "He'd planned to bring the letters along on this trip, explain what he'd started—a relationship with a woman named Kim—and cajole me into calling her. Once we were settled in your kitchen and he discovered that you and Kim were one and the same, well, you know the rest."

"I thought that child had fear written all over his face!" Kate managed.

"Not without good reason. The boy is in a lot of trouble," Chase said wryly. "He didn't have any time to soften up his old man before he had to reveal what he'd done." He gave Kate an odd look. "And it was you who convinced him to come clean immediately."

"Me?" Kate squeaked. Then the memory of her conversation with Nathan came back to her.

"He said you told him he should share whatever was bothering him with me. That a child should tell his parents about the problems he's having. If you hadn't talked to him, I think he might have dropped the whole thing."

Oh, great. If she'd kept her mouth shut, C.G. would have faded away without another word. As it was...

"Me and my big mouth," Kate muttered. "I gave him this wonderful lecture about having a loving father who'd want to know what was bothering him. I never dreamed—"

"Obviously."

Kate glanced sharply at Kincaid. The anger was still there, like smoldering coals in those amber-flecked eyes.

Before he could lash out at her again, before he could bring up the content of that last, vituperative letter she'd written to him—and unwittingly *about* him—there was something more she needed to know.

"But the letters he sent!" she stammered. "They were so beautifully written. I can hardly believe someone Nathan's age could have composed them." With an excited shiver she remembered the letter that had intrigued her so.

Kincaid's bronze skin darkened with an embarrassed flush. "Little thief. He admitted getting into his mother's things and taking some of the letters she'd saved from our...courtship. They were in the attic and I doubt Amy even remembered she had them. He prefaced them with words of his own and retyped parts of my letters to create new ones." Chase grimaced. "Nathan didn't spare any time or expense to himself to come up with this bit of bogus correspondence."

"Oh." So that was the explanation for the odd, patchwork quality of the letters, Kate mused. Then, unthinking, she blurted, "But one was a love letter!"

Kincaid's gaze dropped to the floor and his shoulders sagged beneath the stiff tweed of his jacket. "It was something I'd written to Amy just before our marriage. I never dreamed she'd still have anything like that around the house." He paused and his voice took on an empty faraway quality. "Not after all we've been through."

Kate experienced an odd jab in her chest, remembering the words of that letter:

> I imagine you rising in the morning, your cheeks rosy with sleep and your hair tumbled about in wonderful abandon, and I cannot wait until I am there to share that moment with you. To awake at your side, to touch...

He must have loved his wife very much then. Perhaps he loved her still. He'd never hinted at what had drawn them apart. The idea of Chase and his no-doubt beautiful wife—Amy, he'd called her—was somehow distressing to Kate. *I have no claims on him,* she reminded herself as she glanced at Kincaid's steely expression. *And I'm going to be fired in a minute anyway.*

Her stomach took a sickening plunge as he stood up and walked around to the front of his desk. He braced himself against the glossy wood and drew his glasses from his coat pocket. Slowly and deliberately he put them on.

His eyes shielded, he inclined his head backward, as if to study her through the lower halves of imaginary bifocals. Kate squirmed and wished she could stand, but Kincaid had her trapped. His body was so close to hers that to stand would mean brushing against him in a way she knew to be unwise—unwise because of the angry, unflinching look on his face. And because of the tight, breathless feeling of desperation and desire in her chest.

"Now that you know how I came into possession of your letters, I'm sure you realize you have some explaining to do."

"Sir?" Kate challenged, resenting Kincaid's clipped, imperative tone.

"The letter. The one in which you called the administrator of your hospital, among other disparaging comments, 'a hard-hearted, unfeeling, uncooperative chauvinist who has been turning a deaf ear to the needs of the nurses in this hospital.' Surely you remember those words, Ms Matthews? They're a very strong indictment, especially if you didn't mean them."

Kate's toes curled inside her white shoes. Every muscle in her body knotted with tension. Finally, in the softest, calmest voice she could muster, she said, "But, Dr. Kincaid, I meant every word."

CHAPTER FIVE

"WHAT?" CHASE BLINKED several times behind his glasses before pulling them off and folding them into his pocket.

Kate smiled grimly. For once Kincaid was at a loss for words.

"Would you like to repeat what you just said?" he asked faintly. "Just for clarification."

"I said that I meant every word I wrote in the letter to C.G.," Kate hurried on before she had time to consider what she was doing. "The evening I wrote that letter I was extremely angry with you. You'd behaved callously and indifferently about something important to me both personally and professionally. I didn't have anyone to talk to and, well, you know the rest."

"Am I to believe, then, that because I think you and Marlis Owens are looking for problems where none exist, you consider me—and I quote—churlish, unreasonable and suspicious? You have a very impressive vocabulary, Ms Matthews. Virulent, but impressive."

Kate winced. She'd forgotten just how scathing her words had been. Yet perhaps her own mistake had been not getting her complaints out in the open sooner. "As I've said before, Dr. Kincaid, the doctors in this hospital—and I'm afraid you might be included in that number—have traditionally not regarded nurses' opinions with a great deal of respect. That was the reason my position as spokesperson for the nurses was created—to give us a voice." Kate sounded much more confident than she felt. Why did he keep looking at her that way? Staring at her with a mixture of amazement, amusement and disbelief?

"And you've certainly been using your new 'voice' to shout from the rooftops," Kincaid remarked dryly.

"Sir?" Kate's brow furrowed. "I've repeated our conversations to no one except those filing the complaints."

"No one? Not even a complete stranger? Some doctor from Chicago whom you knew only by his initials?"

Kate blushed. "I was venting my frustrations, not—"

"Did it occur to you that this C.G. might *know* the administrator at St. Mike's? Or enjoy spreading the news that this 'volatile, unpredictable and difficult' man was making life miserable for a whole host of nurses back in North Dakota?' Kincaid's voice had grown ominously low, as close to a growl as Kate had ever heard.

"No. It didn't."

"And I suppose it didn't occur to you that speculating about a man's private life is totally out of line?"

It was the hint of sarcasm that infuriated her.

"No. It didn't. The letter was merely a means of venting my frustrations. I was angry." Her chin came up defiantly and she stared straight into the depths of amber, green and gold. "Justifiably angry. Until you seriously consider the nurses' requests, I have to believe that you consider us second-class citizens within this hospital."

"I believe you've behaved rather 'second-class' in this instance, Ms Matthews. Or at least 'second-rate.'"

Kate gasped sharply, as though she'd been slapped. Her cheeks stung with anger and humiliation. "How dare you—"

"How dare I what, Ms Matthews?" His voice was cold. "*I'm* not the one who's out of line here. Perhaps I should be grateful to my son for what his prank has revealed."

Kincaid drew himself to his full height and Kate shrank down in her chair.

Perhaps it was wrong to have written what she did to C.G., but it was also true. Could Kincaid fault her for telling the truth? And those letters from C.G. had seemed so compassionate, so human, so unlike the man before her now.

She stood quickly and with such force that the calves of her legs pressed back against the chair and made it totter. "I won't take any more of this, Dr. Kincaid. Unless you have something either productive or professional to say to me, I'd like to leave now."

He arched one eyebrow and said, "It seems you'll do just as you like, regardless of what I want, Ms Matthews."

Kate gave him the stare she'd used more than once to humble her rowdy brothers. "And I'd like you to remember that, Dr. Kincaid. This is one nurses' spokesperson who won't back down under your bullying."

"Bullying?" Kincaid muttered. "Bullying?" He moved toward her, but Kate didn't wait to see what he would do. She was already on her way out of the office.

"IF IT GETS ANY WORSE, I'm going to quit," Molly announced to Kate. They were sprawled across Kate's couch and love seat respectively, dressed in shorts and halters, listening to the grating of the air conditioner as it choked out a stream of air too weak to cool the small apartment.

"It's the heat, that's all. Everyone's grumpy." Kate moved one leg to find an unwarmed section of cotton upholstery.

"Is that what Kincaid's been lately? Grumpy? That's like calling World War II a skirmish! That's like calling the Pacific Ocean a puddle. That's like calling—"

"Okay, so he's been *really* grumpy," Kate groaned. "I don't want to talk about Kincaid tonight." *Or think about him*. She rolled off the couch. "Want a hot dog?"

"Nothing hot. Not even a dog. Let's go get a banana split—without the hot fudge. That's the only supper I want."

Kate didn't feel like cooking, anyway. Between the scorching weather and the ongoing mental battle she was waging about Kincaid, she hadn't slept much in the past two days. Listlessly she poked her feet into some ragged slides that looked more like bedroom slippers than sandals. "Come on, then," she said to Molly.

"Do I need to change?" Molly asked, woefully tugging at the back hem of her cutoffs. "These are awfully skimpy shorts."

"No worse than mine," Kate pointed out, "and I'm not putting on one more inch of clothing. Nobody's going to see us or care."

"Famous last words," Kate thought to herself after they pulled into the Dairy Queen and queued up in a long line of children waiting for soft-serve relief from the heat. They hadn't been there two minutes when Chase Kincaid, Nathan and Emily rode up on matching bikes.

Kate groaned aloud. Here she was, in shorts that measured less than twelve inches from waist-band to hem and a halter that could double as a headband. Kincaid would think her entire wardrobe fit in a shoebox if he kept running into her dressed like this.

Chase, on the other hand, looked as if he'd just come from a modeling shoot for men's summer clothing. His pants were pale peach, his short-sleeved shirt a plaid of the same hues with a dark green stripe. His crisp blond hair was combed away from his face, revealing the high intelligent curve of his forehead and the faint bronze of his skin.

"He is gorgeous," Molly commented into Kate's ear. "Too bad the personality doesn't match the body!"

Kate averted her eyes. Perhaps Kincaid wouldn't notice them.

No such luck. "Kate! Kate! Hello!" Emily yelled at her across the parking lot.

Kate gave a weak wave. It was enough for Emily. She towed her father and brother toward them with the enthusiasm of a tugboat heading for port.

"Hi! Isn't it hot? Dad said we could have anything we wanted for supper. I'm having a malt. How about you?"

Kate struggled to focus her attention on the children, but her gaze kept wandering to Chase. He hadn't even said hello, but that was typical since their nasty showdown in his office. Self-consciously she tugged on her halter top, which was creeping upward.

"A banana split, I think."

"Yum. Maybe I'll have that instead. Come on, Nathan, let's go read that big menu on the side of the building and see what else they have." As quickly as she'd come, Emily disappeared, magically taking Nathan and Molly with her.

Kate shifted from her right foot to her left. Finally she noticed the beginnings of a smile pulling at the corners of Chase's mouth.

"Is something funny?" She hadn't meant to sound argumentative and hoped that wasn't how he'd interpreted her question.

He considered her for a moment before saying, "I was just thinking that with the amount of money you earn, you could buy some bigger clothes."

Kate could feel the blush spread from the top of her forehead all the way to her toes. Chase could see it, too.

"I didn't think I'd run into anyone I knew." Her hand went to the front of her halter top.

"Obviously."

"It's very warm out, you know," she said defensively, pleased that he'd noticed her, yet unaccountably distressed at his very male reaction.

"And if you wear things like that, every man within a ten-mile radius is going to be even warmer."

This time she joined him in a smile. "I guess I can't do anything you'll approve of," she challenged mildly.

His eyebrow slid up in a seductive arch. "Oh, I approve of the clothes, Ms Matthews. No matter what else you do."

Before she could decipher his meaning, Emily and Nathan returned with their purchases, Molly strolling not far behind.

As Chase turned to leave, Emily paused in front of Kate. "Can Nathan and I come and see you sometime, Ms Matthews? We don't have many friends here yet. Would you mind?"

What could she say? The surprise and apprehension on Chase's face only urged her on. "Of course. Any time. I'd like that."

Kate could see the disapproving set of Chase's shoulders as the trio retreated, but a satisfied smile settled on her face. She was furious with Chase Kincaid—and he with her—but despite the terrible words they'd exchanged, she still remembered those letters Nathan had pirated—beautiful, loving letters. Kate was as curious as ever about Chase Kincaid, the man. Perhaps a visit with his children would answer some of her questions.

"TROUBLE ON FLOOR FOUR coming up," Molly intoned as she glided toward Kate the next morning.

"What's that supposed to mean?" Kate asked calmly, accustomed to Molly's dramatics.

"This." Molly pointed to the new-patient list. "Four new patients, three of whom belonged to Dr. Nash."

Kate groaned inwardly. That was trouble. She'd been lucky enough to avoid doing rounds with Nash ever since she'd reported him to Kincaid. Now there was no escaping it.

"Just my luck, I—"

The chart she was holding slipped from her fingers, landing on the floor with a clatter. Kate stopped to retrieve it, then rose to the greeting: "Clumsy today, Ms Matthews? Bad trait in a nurse."

Kate held onto her temper and her tongue. She'd expected Ardon Nash to be cool toward her, but not outright hostile.

The doctor had the look of a man put together by a committee. All the parts were adequate, but none of them quite fit. He was balding, with a fringe of pale brown hair, which he kept long. It brushed at his collar in the back, reminding Kate of the dust ruffle on her bed. His nose was short and wide, the nostrils pinched up slightly in a perpetual flare. Ferdinand-the-Bull nostrils, Kate thought absently. And they were twitching with irritation.

"Are you ready for rounds, or do you plan to stand there gawking all day?"

"Ready, Doctor. Whenever you are." Kate gave the cart a push and followed it from behind the desk. "Your patients are in—"

"I know where my patients are."

Kate breathed deeply. Stay calm, she reminded herself. She managed to smile serenely through his subtle barbs in the first two rooms, but by the time they reached the third room, her control on her temper was wearing thin.

'Nurse, see that this patient is given…' and Nash spewed out a string of medications long enough to make a pharmacist's head whirl.

"Could you put that order in writing?" Kate handed him the patient's chart.

"You heard me. You aren't deaf."

"I prefer not to take a verbal order, sir. If you'd just—"

"Are you refusing to follow my instructions?" Nash's face flushed and the raspberry-colored patch bled across his forehead.

"We're not to follow oral instructions, Dr. Nash. I'd be happy to—"

He clamped his pen to the chart. "I'd like to have a word with you in the hall, Nurse Matthews."

Here it comes. Kate steeled herself for a tongue-lashing.

"I don't like being second-guessed or corrected in front of my patients," Nash began, his voice thick with anger. "And I won't allow any high and mighty female—"

"Good day, Dr. Nash, Nurse Matthews." Kincaid seemed to materialize from nowhere.

"Same to you, Dr. Kincaid." Nash's manner did a sudden one-hundred-and-eighty-degree turn. Kate watched, fascinated, as he turned a beaming smile on Kincaid. "Dr. Kincaid," he continued, "I had a question for you concerning..." He moved into step with Chase, his reprimand and Kate forgotten.

Kate stared at their retreating backs. Was it an accident that Kincaid had appeared so opportunely? Or was her hunch correct—that he'd been silently monitoring the situation between her and Nash?

She gathered up the charts and headed back to the nurses' station. "Did you see that?" she asked Molly.

"See what? Nash chasing Dr. Kincaid down the hall like he was a long-lost school chum?'

"That's it. He was busy lambasting me for not taking a verbal order one minute and—"

"—hanging onto Kincaid's every word the next."

"I can't figure that guy out," Kate said. "Whatever made Nash feel compelled to even consider a career in medicine?"

"Money," Molly said flatly. "What else?"

"I don't think that's why Dr. Kincaid is a physician," Kate pointed out softly.

"No, not Kincaid," Molly agreed. "Even though I've been in plenty of trouble with Kincaid, I see something truly compassionate in him. He really loves his work."

Kate nodded. She felt the same way. No matter how harsh Chase had been with her, she didn't doubt his compassion for someone who was suffering. Chase would be a doctor if it *cost* him to be one. If only he'd save a little of that charity for his nurses . . .

Kate was still perturbed when Nathan and Emily accosted her just outside St. Mike's in the new employees' parking lot.

"Hello, Ms Matthews! How are you?"

"Emily! What are you doing here? And Nathan?" Kate smiled at the gangly but attractive pair before her.

"Waiting for Dad. Have you seen him?" Nathan had barely spoken to her since the bogus-letter incident. Kate was pleased to see that he'd finally recovered from his embarrassment.

"No, but I'm sure he'll be out soon if he knows you're waiting."

"We're going to buy a house today. Isn't that exciting?" Emily's eyes were bright with enthusiasm.

"You are? Where?"

"Not very far from your house. Walking distance, I think. Then we can visit each other whenever we want."

Kate registered that bit of information with some dismay. Kincaid within walking distance? The idea alarmed her, but she felt a small, undeniable surge of pleasure, too. Why was it that whenever Kincaid was involved, she felt pulled in two directions? Having him nearby would have been wonderful—if he weren't the administrator at St. Mike's.

Then Emily glanced over Kate's shoulder and began to wave. "Over here, Dad. We're with Ms Matthews."

Kate winced. She wasn't having much luck avoiding anyone today. She felt rather than saw Chase come up beside her.

"Are you kids ready?"

"Of course," Emily answered, her whole face beaming. "I told Kate we're going to buy a house in her neighborhood."

"Not in her neighborhood, exactly..."

"But close by. Close enough so we can visit. Right, Kate?"

Kate nodded. What else could she do? These children had no inkling of the discord between her and their father.

"Ms Matthews has other things to do than visit with you two," Chase reminded Emily. Kate heard the warning in his voice, but if his daughter did, she chose to ignore it.

"Oh, I know, but I'm sure we'll be great friends," Emily announced confidently.

"I'm sure we will," Kate murmured, unable to help herself. The child's enthusiasm was contagious.

"Don't worry," Chase said when Emily was out of earshot. "My children won't be bothering you."

"They're no bother," Kate replied. "I like your children."

"That's surprising," Chase observed coldly, "considering the contempt you display for their father." Before Kate could comment, Chase had herded the pair into the car and driven away.

Kate closed her eyes and willed away the pain that was beginning to throb in her temples. Why had she ever written that stupid letter? It had ruined everything between them. Worse yet, it had damaged her working relationship with the one man who could keep Dr. Ardon Nash in line. The pain in her temples increased. Kincaid and Nash. Between them, they were going to drive her crazy.

AT THREE-THIRTY the next afternoon, Marlis Owens slammed the dressing-room door so hard that a picture shuddered off the wall and fell to the floor.

Kate glanced up sharply from the bench where she was seated, tying the laces of her tennis shoes in a double knot. "What's wrong? Student revolt?"

Marlis gave a loud unladylike snort. "There will be if things don't change pretty soon. And I'll be leading it!"

"Tell me more." Kate stretched out her long bare legs.

"I'm going to make a Dr. Nash doll and stick it so full of pins he'll look like a homemade Christmas ornament. Voodoo, that's what I'll use. He'd look good as a shrunken head, that inconsiderate, rutting creature. The smaller the better. Then it might be the right size to hold his brain. That—"

"Whoa! I think you'd better tell me what happened." Kate had a sinking sensation in the pit of her stomach.

Marlis flopped onto the bench next to Kate. "You know Wendy Rogers, don't you? That new girl—big eyes, frail, really somber?"

Kate nodded. The poor girl always looked scared half to death, obviously intimidated by the size of St. Mike's.

"Dr. Nash got her in a corner today and read her the riot act for some infraction or other. Poor thing nearly died of fright. And then do you know what he had the gall to do?" Marlis's face was rigid, her hands clenched. "He told her he knew a way she could ensure getting good grades."

"You're kidding, right?"

"'Fraid not. He also told her he was the man who could help her get them."

"Creep!"

"It took me half an hour to get Wendy to actually tell me what happened," Marlis said, her voice trembling with outrage.

Kate dropped her head into her hands and moaned. Why this? Why now?

"You'll talk to Kincaid, of course?" Marlis asked.

"If you file a complaint," Kate answered wearily. "Unless you think it won't happen again..." She suggested without much hope.

"Does the sun rise in the east?" Marlis muttered. "Does it set in the west? Nash has been a nasty lecher for too long. Someone needs to tell him to cool it!"

It was easy for Marlis to say, Kate thought. But who was going to be stuck with the job of telling Kincaid about this? She was. Even if Kincaid handled it as discreetly as he had the improperly medicated patient, Nash would be angered by her interference. She sighed. Where was Molly anyway? What she needed right now was a good fast game of tennis. If she imagined that the tennis ball was Nash's head, she should be able to win hands down—and get rid of a little steam, as well.

"Sorry I'm late," Molly gasped, bursting through the changing-room door with hurricane force. "I had to talk to Dr. Kincaid, and he and Dr. Nash were having a big powwow, so I had to wait...." Her voice became muffled as she stuck her head into a locker.

Kate remained silent. Nash wasn't stupid, she thought. He was ingratiating himself with Kincaid just in case.

She was grateful for Molly's constant chatter as they drove to the tennis courts. Whatever took her mind off Chase—even Nash and the hospital—was a blessing these days.

As they were doing warm-up stretches, a familiar voice floated through the air. "Kate! Hi! Are you going to play tennis, too?"

Emily Kincaid. And Nathan. Both children were dressed in regulation whites and carried expensive Prince rackets. This was obviously not the first time they'd been on a tennis court.

"Hi, kids. I didn't know you played."

"We've taken lessons every year since we were little," Nathan explained. "And played in a league on Saturdays."

"Dad's coaching us this year," Emily added. "We haven't had time to find an instructor yet. Maybe next month he'll have one lined up."

Kate sighed despairingly. If that meant what she thought it did, Chase Kincaid would be driving up any second now and the therapeutic value of her game with Molly would be lost. Almost before the thought was formulated, she heard the slamming of a car door.

"Dad! Over here! With Kate!"

Kate glanced around frantically for Molly, who'd wandered over to the ball machine and was lobbing back the balls it spewed out. Once again, Kate had to face Chase without any moral support.

"Ms Matthews." His voice was cool and distant. "We seem to travel the same paths these days."

"Yes. I guess so," Kate acknowledged inanely, taken with the lean, muscular line of his legs below the pristine white tennis shorts. She remembered the photo Nathan had included in that other letter—the thick, hard chest muscles, the smooth bronze skin, the lightly furred and tapered torso...

Kate gave herself a mental shake. No matter how much she was physically attracted to the man, she had to remember that theirs was a purely professional relationship.

Kincaid obviously had no trouble remembering it. Why should she?

Kate bent over to pick up her tennis racket, unconsciously displaying an attractive sweep of long legs. When she stood up, Kincaid turned away abruptly and began slapping tennis balls to the far side of the court.

A fine gleam of sweat soon broke out on his forehead. He was warming up with more intensity than necessary, Kate thought. Glossy perspiration made him shine like a golden boy in some men's magazine, all slick and powerful.

Kate flicked her tongue along the smooth line of her lower lip.

Chase's blond hair refused to stay out of his eyes, repeatedly flopping over his brows. Impatiently he shook it away. Kate's fingertips itched to brush back those blond strands and skim across his forehead....

Appalled by her thoughts, she angrily chastised herself. Looking neither to the right nor the left, she began to shoot a barrage of balls toward the opposite court. She wouldn't let Kincaid's presence ruin her game. He wouldn't, couldn't distract her. Not a bit.

Still, Molly beat her soundly.

As Kate and Molly were threading their way through the parking lot back to the car, Emily caught up with them. "Kate," she called breathlessly, "could I ask you something?"

"Sure, honey. What is it?" Kate liked Chase's children. They had inherited all of his warmth and good looks with none of his dour intensity. She couldn't help returning Emily's smile.

"I-I know it's a lot to ask," Emily stammered, "but Dad said I could decorate my own room in the new house and...would you, if it wouldn't be too much trouble...but if it is I'll just...but it would be awfully nice if..."

"Get to the point, honey," Kate said, laughing gently. "What is it you want?"

"Help me shop? Help me pick out the curtains and bedspread? I loved your house, Kate. I want my room to be as neat as yours!"

Kate's heart lurched as she looked at the thin, hopeful-eyed girl. "I'd love to. Thank you for asking me."

She was rewarded with a huge grin and a hug. Then Emily whirled around and loped back toward her father and brother.

Molly gave a low whistle.

"What's that supposed to mean?" Kate demanded.

"Nothing. Nothing." Molly rolled her eyes heavenward in mock innocence. "It's just so *refreshing* to see you playing mommy to Dr. Kincaid's—"

"I'm not playing mommy to anyone. Emily and I are friends!" Kate said too forcefully.

"Okay, okay." Molly beat a verbal retreat. "Forget I ever mentioned it! It's just too bad you don't get along with those kids' father as well as you do with them, that's all."

Kate certainly couldn't argue with that. She and the Kincaid children had shared a bond of friendship from the start. She and Chase, well, they'd also experienced something from the very first—but it certainly wasn't friendship.

THE MORNING AFTER Kate's tennis match with Molly, Marlis had already typed up her complaint. It was waiting in Kate's mailbox when she arrived at the hospital.

"I don't want to take this in to Kincaid," she told Molly. "He's going to explode."

"At you?" Molly snorted. "That's unreasonable. It's Nash who's acting like an old billy goat."

"I know, but he has a hard time accepting that Nash is fool enough to behave this way. Kincaid never would. Therefore, neither would any of his staff." Kate scraped her hair from her eyes. "Besides, I represent the pressure of all the nurses' demands. The hospital board is coming at him from one direction, insisting that he put the operation in the black this fiscal year, and we're coming at him from the other side asking for more authority, more responsibility..."

"...more wages?"

Kate shrugged. "Can you blame him for feeling pressured? I wouldn't want to see me, either."

Molly nodded. "I've heard that the board promised Kincaid that if he could put things on track here, they have a donor willing to give enough money to build a new geriatric wing the likes of which you won't see from Chicago to Seattle. It's the carrot they dangled in front of Kincaid's nose to get him to come here in the first place."

Chase loved his work in geriatrics. No wonder he cared so much that things stay on an even keel. Kate sighed. She stood between him and his goal.

If she did her job as spokesperson for the nurses, she would cause Chase trouble. And if she kept quiet...well, she couldn't do that. Whatever attraction she felt for Chase Kincaid would have to be sacrificed until her professional responsibilities were met. And by then, Kate mused, he'd probably dislike her so intensely that neither of them would remember the sparks that seemed to fly between them whenever they were together.

Her best course would be to put all thoughts of Chase Kincaid from her mind, especially during her nonworking hours, but his children seemed set on making that impossible. Proof came with an early Saturday-morning phone call.

"Kate? This is Emily. Can you go shopping with me today?"

Kate rolled over in bed and yawned. What time was it, anyway? Not even eight o'clock. "Honey, the stores don't open for two hours yet!"

"But I wanted to make sure I caught you before you made some other plans. Dad's taking Nathan to a radio-controlled model airplane show. I didn't want to go if there was a chance we could go shopping. Is there?"

So Chase would be away all day. That was good. She and Emily could have their fun without his grim silences spoiling everything. "Sure. Why not? I might even buy something for myself."

"Great! What time should I be over?"

Kate chuckled. "Not for two or three hours—please."

It was ten-fifteen when Emily appeared at the door, dressed in a short denim skirt with a bright yellow blouse, socks, earrings and hair bow. She looked as though she'd stepped off the pages of a teen magazine.

"Don't you look nice!" Kate exclaimed. She'd chosen snug faded jeans and a sloppy oversize shirt, and her hair was caught in a ponytail made with a banana clip.

"And you could be my sister," Emily announced. "Love your clothes!"

There was a definite female influence somewhere in Emily's life. She was already a little clotheshorse. Cautiously she asked, "Emily do you and your mother do a lot of shopping together?"

"Too much!" the girl admitted cheerfully. "Daddy says he's going broke." A frown flitted across her face. "When he says it to me, it always sounds like a joke, but when he says it to Mom, he sounds serious."

Kate bit her bottom lip. This was a subject she didn't dare pursue. Maybe, as he'd implied, Chase did have a legitimate reason for being so suspicious of women's motives. Maybe... She shook her head. Today was Emily's day—and hers. She wouldn't allow thoughts of Chase to intrude.

At five that afternoon Kate declared the day a success. The back seat of her car was piled high with pillows, bedspread, curtains, shams and dust ruffle in a pale, frothy yellow. Once Emily announced that she had a jade-green carpet, there was no doubt in Kate's mind how the room should look. They'd searched all day for the perfect accessories and found a series of posters in jade and yellow, breaking only for a lunch of ice-cream cones and candy bars. They were both exhausted.

"Can you come to my house now, Kate? So we can start decorating?"

Kate thought of Chase, who'd probably arrived home already. "No. Not tonight."

"Oh, please! It would be so much fun." Emily gave her a wistful glance. "And then maybe you and Dad could visit. Nathan and I would like it if you two became friends."

So even the children had noticed the discord between them.

"Maybe some other time, honey."

"Next Saturday? Nathan and I could cook dinner."

Kate tried to hide her dismay. This was all she needed. She and Chase were barely speaking and his children were plotting to bring them together.

"No, Emily. I'm sorry. Your dad and I prefer to keep our relationship purely professional. It's best that way."

The child's disappointment was evident. "Would you come if Dad weren't home?"

"Maybe sometime."

Emily brightened. "Okay. I'll remember that."

Kate smiled as she dropped the girl off at the curb. Her eyes traveled to the large bay window at the front of the house and immediately lighted on Chase. His outline shimmered through the silky drapery at the window where he stood. Was he just waiting for his daughter? Or was he watching Kate?

CHAPTER SIX

"YOU NEED TO GET OUT MORE, Katie, my dear," Molly announced. She paused dramatically while stirring the pot of spaghetti sauce on Kate's stove. "All work and no play is making you a dull girl."

"Gee, thanks," Kate muttered as she set the table for two. "I needed that."

"You have to depend on your friends to tell you the truth, Kate." Molly swung around and wiped her hands on the borrowed apron she'd tied to her waist. "You've been absolutely out of touch with the world all week long!"

Kate wanted to deny Molly's accusation, but she knew it was true. Between the furor over the letters and the tension of working with Dr. Nash, she *was* overwrought and overtired. She suspected that Nash had centered all his frustrations about the complaints, the student nurses—and even his patients—on a single scapegoat. Her. And the strain was beginning to tell.

Even worse for Kate's already battered self-esteem, Chase wasn't speaking to her except when it was absolutely necessary. She wiped her hand across her forehead and brushed away the damp golden strands that had fallen into her eyes.

"It's just been a tough week, that's all. You have those once in a while, don't you?"

"Not like this. I've never had both the hospital administrator and a staff doctor mad at me at once." Molly screwed her face into a comical frown. "And I was sure that if it ever did happen to anyone, it would be me, not you."

Kate chuckled humorlessly. "I'd gladly trade places with you, Molly, if that were possible. But for the time being, I just don't see what can be done."

"You need a diversion. Something to get your mind off work. A date. A movie. Anything!"

It was an old song, Kate thought. Molly had been singing it as long as they'd known each other, and she'd been particularly insistent about it this week. Kate knew she'd have to watch her temper or she'd flare up at Molly, who was, after all, only trying to make helpful suggestions.

"Let's drop it. The spaghetti's done and the bread's warm. I need food more than dates tonight."

"Food more than dates? That just goes to show, Kate, you've lost all perspective. Who wouldn't trade a loaf of bread for a gorgeous man? Why, I've never—"

Kate was grateful for the interruption caused by the ringing of the telephone. Eagerly she reached for the receiver.

"Hello, Kate?" a small voice asked. "This is Emily Kincaid."

"Hello. What can I do for you?" Kate smiled into the phone. Emily and Nathan had virtually adopted her as their best "older" friend and often appeared on her doorstep just when she was at her lowest. Inevitably they brightened her day. The children combined all their father's most appealing qualities—with none of the conflict.

Nathan was still quieter than his sister, but he, too, had become much more open, and he seemed to enjoy the banter that Kate and Emily carried on.

"Nathan and I aren't going to Chicago this weekend like we'd planned."

"Oh?" Kate murmured. "Can you speak a little louder?" It was difficult to concentrate on the conversation with Molly doing her personal version of a rain dance near the phone.

"If it's a man, say yes!" Molly was mouthing. "Say yes!"

"So Nathan and I were wondering if you'd like to come to our house for dinner on Saturday night."

"Say ye-e-e-s!"

Kate gave Molly a fierce look and returned her attention to the phone. "Oh, I don't think so. Not this weekend."

Molly flapped her hands in protest, indicating that Kate was out of her mind.

"Daddy's not going to be home. That's why we'd like you to come. It would be nice to have company, Kate," Emily pleaded.

"But where—"

"To a dinner meeting with some doctor who's flying in from out of town. Dad planned it while he still thought we'd be going home to see Mother this weekend. It'll be just us. You and Daddy won't have to fight about those dumb letters of Nathan's. He won't be around at all."

Across the room, Molly was nearly standing on her head with excitement. "Is it a date?" she whispered loudly. "For heaven's sake, accept!"

Kate sent a quelling stare in her friend's direction. So Molly wanted her to go out, did she? With a man? Would it matter that the "man" was thirteen years old and his eleven-year-old sister would be along? Kate smiled grimly. She had no intention of telling Molly who this "date" really was. That way, she'd have Molly off her back for a few days. And she did enjoy the Kincaid children. It was only their father she found it difficult to be around.

"I'd love to have dinner with you on Saturday night," Kate acquiesced. "Any special time?"

"Seven," Emily said, giggling happily. "This is super! It gets really quiet here without Dad."

"About that..." Kate began.

"Oh, we won't tell him you're coming. And you can go home before he gets back," Emily assured her. "That way you won't have to give each other all those dirty looks."

"Sounds great," Kate murmured into the phone. "See you then."

"'Bye, Kate. I'm glad you're coming!"

Kate couldn't help smiling as she settled the receiver into its cradle. Those kids were really something. A sigh escaped her lips. If only... But *if only*s didn't make things different. *If only*s couldn't change the fact that she and Chase were poles apart in their thinking and their attitudes. The only common ground they shared was Nathan and Emily—and, of course, the hospital. And for Kate, the hospital was rapidly degenerating into a battlefield.

Before she could contemplate further, Molly squealed, "You did it!"

"Yes, Molly, I did. I accepted a dinner invitation for Saturday night."

"Good girl!" Molly approved. "Now who—"

"Don't be so curious," Kate responded coyly.

"Oh, for heaven's sake," Molly muttered, but just then the spaghetti sauce started to boil over the kettle's rim and she forgot entirely about Kate's mysterious date. It wasn't until after Molly had eaten and departed that Kate realized she'd escaped having to tell her friend any lies about Saturday's date.

AT SIX-FIFTEEN, Kate gave one last twirl in front of the full-length mirror inside her bathroom door. She wore a simple sundress of a wonderfully silky fabric that rode on her skin like a breeze. The khaki-green color made the paleness of her complexion and the hazy golden blond of her hair look bright and pure. Kate smiled at herself in the mirror and was pleased with the woman who smiled back.

She was treating this evening like a date, even though she was sharing it not with a man but with the Kincaid children. She wore a fine gold chain around her neck and another at her wrist. Her feet glimmered in gold sandals, and as she moved, the soft rustle of the dress whispered in her ears. It felt good to dress up. She'd spent too many days in nurses' white and too many nights in faded denim jeans. Perhaps Molly was right.

The Kincaid house, located only a few blocks from her own, was of the same vintage as hers, but smaller. It had been beautifully kept up and the lawn was groomed to an almost painful neatness. Obviously Chase was meticulous in every aspect of his life.

The absence of his car in the driveway and the open garage door signaled that he'd already left for his appointment. Kate gave a gusty little sigh. She'd never sneaked into a man's house before or out of one, but that was how this felt—like a clandestine little rendezvous behind the landlord's back.

What did it matter? She and the Kincaid children were friends. Chase hadn't put a stop to that even after he'd discovered Nathan's correspondence with her. To Kate's way of thinking, that was as good as giving his approval. She drew a breath, stepped to the door and pressed the bell.

She certainly hoped the children were right about their father's being out all evening so that she could relax and enjoy the entertaining duo who'd invited her.

"Hi." Nathan stood at the screen door, dressed in blue jeans and a faded sweatshirt.

"Hi, yourself." Kate said lightly. She felt overdressed.

Emily came up behind her brother, wiping her hands on the gingham apron she'd borrowed from Kate. "I just finished cutting up the carrots and celery, Nathan. Did you set the table—Oh, hi, Kate. Come on inside."

The girl was also in jeans and a sweatshirt, hardly appropriate dress for a dinner party, even a small one, Kate thought. But if the children weren't dressed for dinner, the house definitely was.

It gleamed from top to bottom, from the antique light fixtures to the vast expanse of highly polished hardwood floors. There were fresh flowers everywhere, vases of irises from the back yard, pansies in tiny bud vases, even geraniums, their clay pots wrapped in florist's foil.

And candles! Every surface glimmered with light. Even the fireplace, empty for the summer, held a dozen thick vanilla candles, their flames dipping and dancing. The fragrance in the room was divine—flowers and vanilla, wood polish and fresh air. Kate inhaled deeply, moved by the effort the children had obviously gone to.

"It's lovely in here," she murmured. "You must have been slaving all day!"

"Actually, Daddy hired a cleaning lady," Emily revealed, forever forthright. "She's been working here all week. We just did the finishing touches."

"Perfect touches, too," Kate said. "Everything looks wonderful." She turned to glance at Nathan. "Is the supper this special, too?"

An odd, guilty look flickered across his features and disappeared. He glanced at his sister before answering, "Steak. Is that okay?"

"And baked potatoes," Emily offered. "They're in the oven."

"Great. I'm starved." Kate was astounded by these two. Whatever had possessed them to go to so much trouble just for her?

"The music!" Nathan spun around and opened the cabinet that housed their father's complicated stereo equipment. At home with the switches and dials, the boy soon had strains of easy-listening filling the air.

Kate hid a grin. They really *were* doing this for her; otherwise, she suspected, the music would have been heavy-metal rather than the soothing melodies she was hearing. She looked expectantly from Nathan to Emily and caught them staring at her as if she'd just landed from Mars. Kate shifted her feet uncomfortably during the awkward silence that ensued. Finally remembering his job as host, Nathan asked, "Would you like to sit down?"

Kate nodded and moved toward a pale blue wing-backed chair. Settling herself on the firm cushions, she gazed around her in delight, astonished that Kincaid had managed to do so much with this house in such a short time. Every piece of furniture seemed expressly made for it.

As if in answer to her thoughts, Emily asked, "Do you like our new furniture? Daddy and a decorator picked it out."

"It's beautiful," Kate said, "but didn't you bring anything from Chicago?"

"Not much," Nathan admitted candidly. "Mom didn't want Dad to take anything out of the house, so he had to buy new stuff."

Kate was immediately sorry she'd asked, but for some reason, she was having difficulty conversing with the children. Normally they were relaxed and open; tonight they were nervous and unusually quiet. All three sat, hands folded in their laps, awkwardly silent.

Suddenly Emily bolted out of her seat. "I hear a car!" she squealed. Nathan tensed in his place.

"Do you think—"

"Maybe."

"What should we—"

"What's wrong?" Kate asked, confused by their odd behavior. "It was probably just a neighbor's car. You weren't expecting anyone, were—" The fine hairs on the back of her neck tingled. Something was going on. "Nathan? Emily? What's happening here?"

Nathan opened his mouth, but before he could speak, Kate heard first the screen door, then a very familiar voice.

"Nate. Em. I'm home." And Chase Kincaid walked into his living room.

"The house looks great," he was saying, "but why all the candles? And did you take every flower in the gar—Kate! I mean, Ms Matthews! What are you doing here?"

Kate looked coldly at the Kincaid children as they stood together near the fireplace. "I could ask you the same question."

"I live here."

He didn't sound angry, Kate noted with relief, just bewildered—like she was. Kincaid dropped into the chair across from hers, leaned back and crossed his leg over the other knee. Then he folded his arms over his chest and skewered his children with a stern and steady gaze.

His suit coat was missing, and his white shirt was wrinkled and rolled to the elbows. There was a smooth layer of golden hair on his forearms, which intrigued Kate mightily, and his shirt, open at the collar, revealed a V-shaped mat of golden hair on his chest. His trousers, obviously a European cut, fit smoothly over his flat belly and down the long lines of his legs to crisp, black leather loafers. Even hot and rumpled, Kincaid looked good.

"All right, you two," he rapped out. "What's going on?"

Nathan found his voice first. "Emily and I are invited to a roller-skating party, Dad. The kids down the block. Mrs. Fitzsimmons will drive us there and back, so we have to be going now."

"Roller-skating!" Kate gasped, sitting bolt upright in her chair. "But what about—"

"Yeah, Dad. We're going to be late if we don't hurry," Emily pointed out. "And you know how much you want us to make friends here."

"But, Ms Matthews is—" Chase began.

"We got everything ready for dinner, Dad. Now you won't have to be alone tonight." Emily gave her father her most engaging smile. "We hate to see you eat alone."

"There're steaks, Dad," Nathan said in a conciliatory tone. "Rib eye. Your favorite."

"And baked potatoes, Emily put in. They should be ready soon."

"Yeah, just steam the asparagus in the kettle it's in."

"And warm the hollandaise sauce in the microwave."

"Hollandaise sauce?" Chase yelped.

"The cleaning lady made the sauce," Emily confessed.

"And there are all sorts of pastries for dessert. We used our allowances to buy them." The twosome slowly backed toward the door.

Suddenly Chase lunged toward them, but with a burst of speed they dashed out. Nathan's voice drifted back to them. "We'll be home late. Midnight or after. 'Bye."

And then the room was very, very quiet.

Kate wished she could just disappear. There she sat, in Dr. Kincaid's living room, dressed for an evening on the town, staring at the furious, convulsed face of her employer.

Finally he spoke, looking grim. "How much did you know about this?"

"As much as you. They told me you had a meeting tonight and that they wanted company for supper." Kate shifted uncomfortably in her chair. "Little monsters," she added under her breath.

Surprisingly Chase chuckled. "I heard that."

Kate gave him a stony stare. "I meant it."

"I'm sure you did." A twinkle of amusement had sprung to his eyes. "Or worse."

"Won't they ever learn?" Kate muttered.

"About matchmaking, you mean?" Chase groaned and sank into his chair again. "Probably not. They have very single-minded parents. It's a genetic flaw. They won't be happy until they see me paired up like something from the ark.''

At his reference to the ark, Kate felt a smile twitch at the corners of her mouth. Poor Chase. After all, he'd sired these connivers; she'd only befriended them. ''Perhaps you're fortunate. Most children fight seeing their parents involved with anyone other than their original spouses.''

''They're smart enough to see that it wasn't working for Amy and me anymore.'' Chase paused before adding, ''Too bad they can't accept that about you and me.''

Kate looked down at her hands, wrapped in a knot in her lap. ''I'm terribly embarrassed. If you can think of an inconspicuous way for me to slink out of here, I'll be glad to go.''

Chase chuckled silently and, fascinated, Kate watched the movement of his stomach muscles. ''I'm a little embarrassed myself. After all, I fathered that pair of con artists. It's not your fault, you know.''

''But I came here.''

''You were coming to visit my children. I appreciate that.'' His eyes grew dark and serious for a moment. ''No matter what our relationship is at the hospital, I do appreciate the fact that you haven't held it against my kids. You've been a good friend to them, Kate. Thank you.''

She bowed her head in acknowledgment. ''I've enjoyed it—until now.''

Chase unfolded himself from the chair and slowly stood up. ''Well, although this is very awkward, I suppose I should do my best to rectify the situation.''

''There's nothing you have to do. I'll just leave now.'' Kate got to her feet as she spoke.

''Can I at least offer you a glass of champagne? I have a hunch there's a bottle cooling on ice somewhere in the kitchen.''

She glanced at him in surprise. Was this the same man who'd been so stiffly formal all week? She hesitated.

He took her hesitation as yes.

When he returned from the kitchen with a chilled bottle of champagne and two glasses, Kate had walked into the dining room. Nathan and Emily had left their touch there, as well. Candles flickered amid an array of crystal and fine china. A single, long-stemmed red rose lay across the center of one plate.

Thoughtfully, Kate ran a finger across the outer petals of the rose. "Lace tablecloth, napkins folded into fans, newly polished sterling," she murmured. "Those kids must have worked all day, housekeeper or not."

Chase's voice was startlingly near her ear when he spoke. "It's rather a shame to waste it."

She turned to read his expression but found it disappointingly impassive. He handed her a champagne flute and his arm brushed hers as he filled her glass.

Kate closed her eyes, suddenly dizzy. He smelled of leather and musk, and of a clean scent, uniquely his. She opened her eyes to announce, "I've got to be going now. I must..."

"Why?"

"Why?" she countered. "Because, well, I just have to."

"You'd planned to have dinner here, hadn't you?"

"Of course, but that was before—"

"The least I can do is feed you." Chase grinned. "Anyway, I've already turned on the broiler and the asparagus is set to steam. If you want to run away after you've eaten, I'll understand."

Run away? Is that what he thought she was doing? Kate considered the possibility in silence. Perhaps it was. That was very unlike her, running away. "I'd love to have dinner here," she said resolutely.

"Good." Chase smiled. "You've put my conscience at ease."

It wasn't his conscience she wanted to soothe, Kate realized with a threatening blush, but it was better than nothing. Aloud, she said, "I'm a nurse, remember? I like making people feel better."

Somehow, from the look in his eyes and the quirk of his mouth, Kate had a suspicion that he'd interpreted her statement for his own amusement. But the impish expression vanished immediately, replaced by a businesslike glance.

"Rare, medium rare or well done?" he inquired.

For a minute Kate was startled. The champagne had already begun bubbling in her brain. She tried to remember the last time she'd eaten. Probably early this morning—half a bagel, or was it half a croissant?—and not nearly enough to soak up the bewitching effects of this alcoholic nectar.

"Rare to medium rare, I guess."

"Good. Me, too," Chase approved. "Makes it easier."

"Dr. Kincaid, I—" she began.

"Call me Chase."

She'd been waiting for those words, but now when they came, she felt as if she'd cheated to get them—cheated, somehow, by being here because of Nathan and Emily's manipulations, not because their father had invited her.

"Chase, then. I'm very sorry. I feel so embarrassed about tonight I hardly know what to say."

"I suggest that we make the best of an awkward situation. What do you think?"

She gave him a grateful nod. He was asking for a truce, and she was more than willing to agree.

Between them, they managed to get Nathan's and Emily's meal to the table. Kate dished the asparagus and sauce onto the plates while Chase served the steaks. As she leaned across the table to place a final delicate spear on Chase's plate, his arm brushed softly against her breast. She drew back to stare at him. Could he sense the bolts of burning-hot sensation that shimmered through her? Maybe not. He seemed unmoved. Had he even realized he'd touched her? Kate was silent as she took her place at the table across from him.

"Steak sauce? Sour cream? Can I get you anything?"

"No. This is lovely. Thank you." She sawed carelessly at the meat, which was so tender it could have been cut with the gentle touch of a fork.

"More champagne?"

Kate nodded. The bubbling wine helped to numb her nervousness. She wished she'd worn a more discreet dress, at least one with sleeves and a back that didn't plunge quite so far toward her waist. Still, Chase had been purely, clinically—and disappointingly—proper.

Molly would be ashamed of her, Kate thought—alone with Chase Kincaid and not trying to chip away the veneer that kept him so aloof.

Kate swirled the last of the champagne in her glass. She was relaxed now. Practically melting. She glanced upward to find Chase studying her.

"Kate?" His voice was a low pleasant growl.

"Yes."

"I have something I'd like to ask you."

"Go ahead."

"Not if you don't want me to. It involves the letters."

The warm, drifting relaxation she'd been feeling instantly fled. "But you said—"

"I know. No talk about that tonight. It's just that I can't get something out of my mind."

"Yes?" She might as well face it, whatever he had to ask. She'd said some pretty nasty things about him in that last letter.

The outside light had dimmed as nightfall overtook them. His features appeared more chiseled than ever in the fading light, emphasized by the flickering candles.

"Why would you put an ad in a Personals column, Kate? It just doesn't seem to—" he searched for the right word "—fit. Are you lonely?"

Kate smiled ruefully. "Molly submitted that ad."

"Molly? Mulgrew? How? Why?"

Kate stretched in her chair with the boneless ease of a cat. "She'd come for dinner one Saturday evening and for a laugh we composed that ad. It was a game." Kate paused. "At least I thought it was."

"So you didn't even know she'd sent it?"

"Not until I got some responses. You can imagine my surprise when the letters came. I thought I'd faint, but I needed to stay conscious to throttle Molly."

Chase chuckled. "I should have known," he murmured. "I didn't think it quite fit your personality to be putting an ad in a Personals column."

"Nor yours."

"But it seemed perfectly logical to my son." Chase shook his head. "I still can't figure out what possessed that kid."

"He loves you, that's all."

"Love? Then why does he keep doing crazy things like that? Like tonight?"

"You said yourself that he was a problem solver. I was one solution to a problem."

Chase nodded. "I suppose you're right. But still—" he looked at her steadily, the amber glint in his eyes accentuated by the candlelight "—he and his sister can't keep throwing us together like two chemicals in a chemistry equation."

"Don't be too hard on him," Kate said, smiling. "After all, I did get a lovely dinner—just like they promised."

"Which reminds me. I make a fairly mean cup of espresso. Would you like to have some with dessert?"

She studied him openly before answering. "You're being an awfully good sport about this—feeding me and all, in spite of our—differences."

Chase got up and walked to her side of the table, then leaned over to take her dinner plate. The folded-up cuff of his sleeve brushed her bare shoulder and Kate shuddered with pleasure.

"I'm not a complete ogre, you know," he murmured softly. "Some people—though few and far between—even say I can be nice."

"Imagine that," she responded, very aware of his nearness, his scent, his touch.

"They—these few people—even say I'm charming."

"Do they."

"Hard to believe, I know." He walked into the kitchen with the empty plates and returned with a platter of lavish pastries.

He disappeared again, leaving Kate to search her emotions for a definition of what she was feeling.

Her hands were shaking, she noticed, as she reached to pluck a petit four from the crystal plate. Kate dropped the sweet and held her hands in her lap, trying to still them. Despite herself, she gave a little gasp when he returned to the room.

"Did I startle you?" he asked.

"A bit. Perhaps I'm just jumpy this evening."

"Espresso?"

"Perhaps I shouldn't."

"Decaffeinated," he assured her, "and we can have it later."

Chase Kincaid seemed to have an answer for everything.

Could he, Kate wondered, explain the powerful surge of attraction she felt for him? It was no good, Kate told herself despairingly. No good at all. By Monday they'd be at each other's throats again. No matter what she did, he wouldn't forget the things she'd written in that last letter. And no matter what she said, she'd still be his adversary when it came to the nurses' needs.

Charm came easily to Chase Kincaid—when he wanted it to. As he sat down across from her and studied her from beneath the thick fringe of his lashes, her throat constricted. She moved slightly, far too aware of her own rapid heartbeat and speeding pulse, her heated skin.

His eyes skimmed her face with almost clinical detachment until they rested at a point just above the swell of her breasts. He lounged back in the chair, apparently as comfortable as she was uncomfortable.

What was he thinking? Kate felt the same way she had that very first day she'd been called to his office for gossiping with Molly. Was he angry? With her? With the children? Or was it something else that made his eyes smoky and unreadable?

When he finally spoke, his words only confused and alarmed her even more.

"Well, then, Ms Matthews. Would you like to come upstairs with me to the bedroom?"

CHAPTER SEVEN

"THE BEDROOM?" Her voice caught in her throat and the words rushed out in a husky whisper.

"Sure. Emily's bedroom. You helped her decorate it, after all, and it looks wonderful. She's very proud of it."

Kate willed the blush that was sweeping across her body to stop, but she felt it heat every inch of her skin. What a fool she was! Imagining for even a moment that Kincaid had meant *his* bedroom! She quickly pushed away from the table, not wanting him to guess how she'd misunderstood his innocent question.

"Sure. I'd love to." Kate slunk after Chase as he led the way up the stairs.

What was wrong with her, anyway? She was acting like an infatuated teenager confronted with her favorite rock idol! Kate glanced up to stare at his back as he ascended the stairs. He was ramrod straight, his shoulders square and wide beneath his shirt. Kate could see the fine wrinkles pressed into the cloth by the back of his chair and the corner of the shirttail, which was threatening to pull away from the confines of his waistband. She was tempted to tuck it back into place.

She dropped her eyes, but only to the smooth, easy motion of his hips as he mounted the stairs. Lord, but he was well built, Kate mused—and she knew plenty about anatomy to support her opinion.

Her reactions were so foreign and so unlike her that they left her breathless. She'd seen enough bodies not to be shocked or thrilled or even interested by them anymore. And she'd convinced herself that no male was worth sacrificing the wonderful freedom and independence she had. Why, then, was her heart pounding like a trip-hammer against her ribs?

When they reached the top of the stairs, Kincaid turned to speak to her. "The workmen just finished here last week. What do you think?"

Kate, thankful that he couldn't read her mind, glanced down the hallway of pale peach and mint green and murmured, "Very nice." Chase threw open the door to Emily's room.

"Well, here it is."

The room was everything Kate had hoped—whimsical and feminine, attractive and cozy. "It's perfect!"

"Emily likes it. Or should I say loves it," he amended.

Kate moved into the jade-and-yellow room. Emily had hung the posters they'd bought, framed in bright yellow laminate, and on her bedside stand she'd arranged a cluster of photographs in gleaming brass frames. Unthinkingly Kate picked up the closest one.

It was of Nathan, Emily, Chase and a very beautiful woman with dark hair and laughing brown eyes. Kate set the photo down quickly.

"That's Amy. The children's mother," Chase said, his voice quiet. "In happier days."

The tone of hurt and confusion that she'd noticed before when he'd mentioned his ex-wife resurfaced. It gave Kate an empty, helpless feeling in the pit of her stomach.

"I'm sorry."

"Don't be. People get divorced all the time these days."

"But it's harder on some than on others."

He shrugged. "I suppose." He said no more, clamping his lips together in a thin, tight line. "Want to see the rest of the house?" he finally offered.

Nathan's room was typically Nathan—full of books and model airplanes and boyish clutter. Kate admired Chase for not apologizing for the disarray.

As if reading her mind, he commented, "I have to operate on the 'kids will be kids' theory or I'd have strung my son up a dozen times by now." He threw her a disarming, youthful smile. "I seem to remember being a handful as a boy myself."

There was only one more bedroom on the second floor, but the door was closed. "I suppose you want to see the rest," Chase said, sounding embarrassed and scraping his fingers distractedly through his hair.

"Only if you want me to." So far, Chase had surprised and pleased her at every turn, and she wondered what to expect next.

"The decorator and I had a parting of the ways at this room," Chase admitted as he placed his hand on the doorknob and slowly twisted it. "She said I wasn't following through with the ambiance of the house."

Kate peeked around the corner of the door and smiled. The decorator was right. Where the rest of the house was definitely turn-of-the-century, Chase's bedroom was more like turn-of-the-*twenty-first* century.

The walls were lined with sleek bookcases filled with art and medical books. There were no lamps, only indirect lighting from soffits and track lights. And there was no furniture, just a floor-to-ceiling open closet with drawer modules, shoe racks and mirrors on one wall, and a king-sized mattress mounted on a large, low platform against the opposite wall.

It was a modern room, fuss-free, functional and clean-lined, a room with a personality like that of Chase himself.

Kate clapped her hands in delight. "It's wonderful!"

"Do you think so?" He seemed pleased by her enthusiasm.

"Sure. What a nice change. Like a little getaway from the more decorative part of the house." Kate's eye told her that he'd spared no expense to get this clean, sparse look.

"That's what I thought, but the decorator wanted ruffles in here." Chase shuddered. "I wouldn't have slept a wink surrounded by ruffles."

The image of Chase, unclothed and sleeping in that bed, made her mouth and lips go dry. Her mind was doing it again—teasing her with ideas she didn't want to have, images she didn't want to see, thoughts she didn't want to think.

She swallowed the thick lump in her throat and glanced at Chase. He stood in the doorway, relaxed, his eyes friendly and impersonal, his mouth curved in a slight smile.

His mind obviously wasn't playing the same game as hers. He had things in perspective, while she was off on flights of fancy. After all, Kate reminded herself, they hardly knew each other—except for the letters. She stared at the back of his head as she followed him down the stairs. *And those letters were written to his wife.*

"An after-dinner drink?" Chase inquired. "Brandy all right?"

"Whatever you're having will be fine." Kate moved through the living room. "Or perhaps I should just be going now. You've really done too much already."

"Nonsense. I never send my guests home early. I'd get a bad reputation as a host."

"Even when the guests are actually your children's?" She busied herself with a paperweight on the end table.

"If they're under sixteen, they go home at ten o'clock." He turned to give her an appraising stare. "Have you had your sixteenth birthday yet?"

"Only days ago," Kate teased.

"Then have a chair. I'll get the brandy."

He was back in a moment, their fingers meeting briefly as he handed her the glass. She rolled the liquid around in the snifter, inhaling the fragrant fumes, hesitating to put it to her lips. When the drink was gone she'd have to leave. Kate found herself wishing she could prolong this evening.

Chase took the wing-backed chair across from her and stared at her over the rim of his glass. The candles were burning low, and outside, the velvety blackness of night had fallen.

Kate kicked off her shoes and curled her legs beneath her, forgetting for the moment all that had happened between them.

"Why did you decide to become a nurse, Kate?" Chase studied her intently. "Anything in particular?"

"I've always had a strong urge to help people. As a child, every time someone in my family was injured, I felt so helpless. I just made up my mind not to feel helpless anymore."

The look of real interest on Chase's face encouraged her to continue.

"My family was rather a rowdy one." Kate smiled at the understatement. "There was always someone getting his head bashed in or a finger jammed. By the time I was twelve I was already officially Nurse Kate. It seemed only right that I go into nursing."

"Tell me about your family."

Kate shook her head. "No, first tell me more about how you became a doctor."

Chase shifted in his chair. He crossed his legs at the ankles and folded his hands, brandy snifter and all, across his stomach. His eyes took on a faraway look. "I'm sure you know more about me than I do about you." His lips quirked in a smile. "Hospital coffee room, the grapevine and all."

Kate felt her cheeks go pink. "But I'd rather have an accurate version."

Chase chuckled. "Fair enough." He gazed out the window into the blackness and his voice softened. "I'd always assumed that I'd be a doctor, but it's hard to explain, really, how I got into geriatrics." He paused. "Sometimes I think our society is so concerned with youth that we don't take time to appreciate the last half of people's lives."

He sipped at the brandy before continuing, "My own parents were older when I was born. I grew up as they grew old. I had to contend with classmates asking me why my grandfather always took me to school and why my grandmother brought cupcakes on my birthday. All of that affected me deeply, Kate. It made me aware of the experience of aging and made me sympathetic to the needs of older people." Then he added, "My parents were the ones who inspired my dream."

"Your dream?" She spoke softly, afraid of shattering the moment.

"A first-class geriatrics department of my own." His eyes brightened and he sat a little straighter in his chair. "I'd like to see a pioneering division that specializes in researching aging—Alzheimer's disease, senility, everything. We could have social workers, educators, specially trained nurses—"

The sound of the clock on the mantel chiming the half-hour startled him. "Sorry." He smiled, a little abashed. "I didn't mean to bore you."

Bore her? How could this man ever bore her?

"More brandy?" Chase stood up and approached her, carrying a crystal decanter.

"No, thank you. I normally don't drink. Tonight's an exception." She giggled, then raised both hands to her mouth, embarrassed.

Chase's eyebrow arched in a question.

"It just occurred to me that the last time I drank this much Molly and I ended up writing an ad for the Personals column in a magazine."

Chase grinned widely and slapped the top onto the decanter with a vengeance. "No more for you, then. I've had enough trouble as it is with your overindulgences. Consider yourself cut off."

Kate nodded happily. She liked Chase the way he was tonight. Very much. *Too* much.

"What's on your mind now? An ad in the *New York Times*?" His face leaned close to hers, and she caught her breath as she stared into his eyes, their amber flecks sparkling.

"I was just thinking how much you sound like your letters tonight."

The sparkles dimmed and his eyes turned wary. "Oh?"

"It's a compliment. The letters Nathan sent were really lovely. Witty. Intelligent. Sensitive." *Like you,* she added to herself.

"Well, I'm glad to hear that. I've wondered exactly what he included. Frankly I've forgotten most of what I'd written." He paused, now on obviously unsteady ground.

"Would you like to read them some day?" Kate offered. "It seems only right."

Relief washed over his features. "I'd appreciate that. Thank you."

"One thing did surprise me," she ventured. "Nathan included one of your...love letters, which was very beautiful, but rather premature, considering how short our supposed correspondence was." Oddly, she found it difficult not to feel jealous of the woman for whom that letter had been written. Kate felt almost compelled to bring up the subject, compelled to discover what he would say about his ex-wife.

"That brings back a very painful time for me." Chase's words were clipped, and he lapsed into silence without further explanation.

He'd said some bitter things about women, Kate remembered. What had made his marriage come apart?

Just then, the telephone rang, dispelling the quiet mood. Chase answered it with an abrupt "hello" and the one-sided conversation that followed made little sense to Kate.

"I see.... You're sure?... You realize that we have to deal with this when you get home.... I don't think... Well I suppose... By ten o'clock. No later."

When Chase returned, he wore a half-amused, half-angry expression. "Nathan strikes again." He sank into his chair with a sigh.

"Nathan? Now what?"

"He called to say that he and Emily were both invited to stay overnight at the Fitzsimmons."

"And?"

"I agreed." Chase rubbed his knuckles across the worried ridge in the center of his forehead. "I shouldn't have. I should have made them both come home and face the music for what they did tonight."

"Why didn't you?"

"I'm not quite sure," he answered slowly. "Perhaps I don't know what I'm going to say to them yet. I'll have to think of a punishment."

"I'm sorry to be the cause of that."

"You aren't the cause. You're the victim."

Kate smiled. "I felt that way earlier, but I truly have enjoyed this evening. You're a wonderful host."

Chase smiled wearily back at her. "Maybe that's why I didn't want them home tonight. I'm not angry enough anymore. I want to be able to breathe fire on them when they get back."

"Then I'm glad I won't be here to see it." Kate stretched, unmindful of the fact that the shoestring strap of her sundress had slipped from her shoulder. "I suppose I should leave before you begin to breathe fire on me."

"I'll save that for the office," he replied wryly. "Tonight we've called a truce. Anyway," he added, "now that the children aren't coming home, you might as well join me in a cup of midnight espresso."

It was too tempting to resist. She waited in drowsy contentment as he brewed the coffee, inhaling the rich scent wafting from the kitchen. The candlelight, the food, the champagne. She felt too utterly relaxed to move.

Their fingers brushed as Chase handed her the cup and saucer. Kate tensed. She shouldn't be feeling like this; she shouldn't be attracted to the one man who had so much power over her professionally. Still, she thought as she studied him from beneath the thick fringe of her lashes, it couldn't hurt to know the enemy, if enemy he were.

Chase settled back into his chair, remaining silent for several moments. When he spoke, his words surprised Kate. "I'm sorry if I sound sharp when the subject of my ex-wife comes up. It's very painful for me."

"I didn't—"

But Chase was not to be put off. "Amy and I had a rather turbulent relationship from the start."

Was he actually going to tell her what had happened between him and his ex-wife? Kate wondered. Nervously she ran her index finger around the rim of her cup.

"Amy never shared my dreams." The statement was bleak, bitter. Chase looked out into the darkness for a long moment before he slowly continued, "We met while I was in pre-med. Amy was studying fashion merchandising at the time. She was very young and beautiful, full of life—and of herself."

So that's where Emily's taste for fashion had come from, Kate deduced.

"It was my naïveté, I suppose, that made me think she really cared about what I was attempting to do. Pediatrics, then geriatrics. Healing." He gave a laugh that was harsh and humorless. "Stupid of me. I suppose I should have seen it from the start."

"Seen what?" Kate asked softly.

"Why she wanted to marry a doctor."

"Because she loved you, I suppose."

He shook his head. "No, not quite. Amy loved the idea of being married to a doctor. It fulfilled a fantasy for her, a childhood dream of what successful women were supposed to do—marry a doctor."

He glanced at the blank look on Kate's face and smiled. "You don't understand because you work with doctors, Kate. You see them through different eyes." He gulped down the last of his coffee. "Amy saw the income, the prestige, the fancy home. She didn't see the other side of the coin—the long hours, the pressure, the fatigue."

"And she didn't like being married to a man whose mind was on his work twenty-four hours a day, seven days a week?" Already Kate could see a clearer picture of the beautiful but immature Amy Kincaid.

"You've got it." He rolled his eyes ceilingward and rested his head against the back of the chair. "She thought the tag M.D. meant 'money on demand.'"

It was an old story, one Kate had often heard before. As Chase had suggested, the idea of being a doctor's wife was frequently more pleasant than the reality. The reality included raising children alone, attending parties solo, inviting guests to dinner only to hear her husband's beeper going just as they sat down to eat. She felt a twinge of guilt. More than once, she'd been the one to call a doctor away from his family.

"Your being summoned away from the dinner table wasn't her idea of fun?"

"Not hardly. It got so that I dreaded mealtimes. I sat poised on the edge of my chair praying I'd get through dessert before the phone rang."

He poured another dollop of brandy into his snifter and swirled it in the bottom of his glass. "It was my fault, too, I suppose. Type A personality and all. I was a workaholic."

"Was?" Kate inquired.

He smiled. "Was and am again. I took a sabbatical from it for a couple of years."

"How does one do that?" Kate tucked her bare feet under her and pushed her hair away from her forehead. "And why?"

"Why?" Chase's brow furrowed. "To make an attempt to save a crumbling marriage. To show Amy I could be an attentive husband. How? By pulling back, I suppose. By limiting office hours, by doing hospital rounds during the day and not at dinner hour. By refusing to work every weekend and holiday."

"And?" Kate was intrigued by Chase's honesty. The distance she'd felt between them was shrinking. Was it the candlelight, the lateness of the hour, the absolute privacy the children had afforded them?

"And then you find out it's not just the long hours and the absences that are causing trouble in the relationship."

Kate stayed silent. If there was one thing she was good at, it was listening. She listened now.

"It's funny, you know," he said softly, more to himself than to her, "but after all the complaining Amy did about my absence, she found it even more difficult to tolerate my presence."

He smiled at the question on Kate's face and went on, "By the time I got around to making time for my family—for Amy—she didn't want me anymore." There was another long empty silence. "If she ever did want me, that is. That's a question I haven't quite answered."

"Chase, you don't have to tell me this."

"I realize that." He uncrossed his legs and crossed them again. "But you're easy to talk to."

"Will you regret it tomorrow?"

"I'm not planning to do anything I'll regret tomorrow." Then he looked at her, his eyes reflecting the dancing candlelight and some emotion she couldn't fathom. "Unless, of course, we finish the third bottle of champagne in the kitchen and all of the brandy." He shrugged. "Then I might do something I'd regret."

A little shiver of pleasure skittered down her spine. At least there was a *potential* attraction between them. It had felt very one-sided to her until now.

"About Amy..."

"Oh, yes." He closed his eyes. "There's not much more to say. She married *Doctor* Chase Kincaid, not Chase Kincaid, that's all. Our values and our dreams were just too different. After a while the physical attraction, sex—no matter how good it is—just isn't enough."

Kate felt a jolt in her midsection. To compose herself she played with her empty espresso cup, turning it round and round on its saucer.

She was jealous! Jealous of a man's sexual relationship with his own wife, of all things! And a man she barely knew, at that. The realization rocked her. Katherine Matthews, "Iceberg" Matthews, feeling gut-wrenching, mind-boggling lust for her employer? It was completely and totally improbable. It was also true.

"Hey!" Chase unfolded his legs and pushed himself straighter in the chair. "I'm sorry. I didn't mean to inflict all of this on you. It's just that—" he studied her curiously "—you seem to listen so well."

"I've had lots of experience." Kate grimaced. "After all, Molly's been my best friend for years. Listening to you is easy."

Chase laughed. She could see his even white teeth and the appealing laugh lines at the corners of his eyes. It struck her again how wonderfully handsome he was. Especially when he laughed.

"Molly, Nathan and Emily. What a trio," he said. "I should punish all of them—but I can't."

"Can't?"

He shook his head. "I've enjoyed tonight too much to be hard on any of them." A grim look flickered across his face. "It's been a long time since I've really talked to anyone. I didn't realize how much I'd missed that."

"I should be going," Kate murmured regretfully. "Even good times have to end."

Chase nodded. "I suppose so."

"And Chase," she added. "You won't hear about your marriage to Amy on the hospital grapevine. Not through me."

"I know. And thank you." He smiled tiredly. "It's probably more common knowledge already than I care to admit, though."

"How can that be?" Kate got up from the too comfortable chair, her brow furrowed. "Of course, I don't exactly hang out in the coffee room."

"Amy was pretty verbal in her complaints about my qualities as a husband," he said dryly. "She complained that I had a mistress—dozens of them, in fact—that she couldn't compete with."

Kate gasped. Chase hardly seemed the philandering type.

"Oh, not that kind of mistress," he corrected. "The old, wrinkled, gray-haired kind."

"But I don't under—"

"Amy always said I loved old women better than I loved her."

Kate remembered the woman in the wheelchair, and for a moment, she understood Amy Kincaid. It would take a woman with a strong sense of self to share a man like Chase with so many others.

As he moved across the room to where she stood, Kate realized how very tall he was. She searched frantically with her toes for her high-heeled sandals.

He stood before her, so close the fabric of his shirt brushed against the front of her sundress. Her toe curled around one shoe and she dragged it toward her. Awkwardly she struggled into the sandal. Chase reached out a hand to steady her, and his strong fingers around her elbow sent shivers of excitement up her arm. Then she slipped into her other shoe and he released her.

"I think perhaps I'll walk home," Kate murmured. "It's so beautiful and that champagne is still buzzing in my brain. The car will be easy to get tomorrow."

"I'll walk with you."

The night was clear and warm with just a slight summer's breeze. They walked along in companionable silence until they reached the porch steps of Kate's apartment house.

"Thanks for staying for dinner once you knew who was cooking."

"Thanks for cooking." She was amazed that her voice could sound so normal when her lips were crying out for his. But that was a fantasy. Kincaid didn't go around kissing his nurses when—

The swift, soft brush of his lips on hers made her gasp with surprise and pleasure.

"Good night, Kate." His voice was low and husky, filled with a longing that seemed to echo her own. Before she could utter a word, he turned and walked swiftly away from her.

As she stood on the steps, staring into the darkness, a wave of aching desire engulfed her. For the first time in many years she'd met a man who stirred a longing within her. For the first time in recent memory, she'd not wanted an evening to end. The realization came with a shock that she, Kate Matthews, had wanted to spend the night with Chase Kincaid.

But of course that was impossible, she told herself. And the reason was obvious. It had been perfectly clear to her all evening that Chase Kincaid was still in love with his wife.

CHAPTER EIGHT

MUCH TO KATE'S disappointment, it was business as usual at the hospital on Monday morning. When she encountered Chase briefly in the hallway, he was friendly but distant, and she saw no sign of the charming, forthright man he'd been two nights before. There was a wall between his professional and private worlds, which he would allow no one to break down.

"Good morning, Dr. Kincaid."

"Good morning." His words were crisp and he kept his eyes on the chart in his hands.

"Nice day."

"Hmm. Yes. Of course." But he was barely aware of her. And when Kate moved silently away, he didn't seem to notice that she'd gone.

"Perk up, Matthews. You look terrible. Are you tired? Or depressed? You weren't fired this morning—were you?" Molly peered closely at Kate's face. "Why the gloomy look?"

"Not gloomy," Kate corrected. "Just tired. I didn't sleep very well the last couple of nights. Tired and... contemplative." She'd hardly slept when she got home after her evening with Kincaid, and all day Sunday she'd been abstracted. By Sunday night she was too keyed up to sleep, despite her exhaustion.

"Oh," Molly's mouth puckered, "big word. What'd you get tangled up with Saturday night? A thesaurus?"

Kate couldn't respond to Molly's banter today. "No, I... well, never mind." She couldn't put it into words. And certainly not to Molly. Yesterday's bittersweet feeling still lingered in her today. Happy. Sad. Pleased. Disappointed. And it all had to do with Chase Kincaid.

She'd lain awake the past two nights mulling over the situation. Things had been far simpler when only their professional conflicts stood between them. But now, after hearing the longing in his voice when he talked about his ex-wife and seeing the sadness in his eyes, she was convinced that Chase still loved Amy. Even through all the hurt he'd suffered, he refused to speak badly of her. What else could it mean but that he still loved her? Chase wasn't ready for another relationship, Kate warned herself. *Go slow. Don't let yourself be hurt.*

"What's wrong with you?"

Kate had forgotten Molly's presence. "Just thinking, that's all."

"Dreaming, you mean. You look all floaty."

"Floaty?"

"Yeah, like you're floating on air. Where did you go Saturday night, anyway?"

"Not now," Kate hissed. She could see Dr. Nash making his way down the corridor.

"He walks like a duck," Molly observed under her breath.

"Shh. He might hear you."

"Frankly I don't care if he does. The old billy goat needs to be put in his—Good morning, Dr. Nash." Suddenly Molly was all professional. Kate turned away to hide a smile. She pulled out the chart cart and turned back to Nash.

"Ready, Doctor?"

"Yes."

Nash was behaving differently this morning, Kate noticed. Quieter, less abrasive. And he couldn't seem to keep his eyes off her. Kate liked the old Nash better.

He was uncharacteristically calm as they did rounds, not barking orders or snapping insults about the "incompetent" staff as he usually did. It seemed almost eerie to Kate. Nash had something on his mind.

"Nurse Matthews, I'd like to speak with you for a moment," he said as they finished with the last of his patients.

"Yes, Doctor?"

"Privately, if you will." He gestured toward an empty room. "We could step in here."

More curious than alarmed, Kate followed him into the room. She stood rigidly just inside the doorway while Nash leaned heavily against a bedside table.

"You and I have some things to discuss."

"Oh?"

"Please don't play the innocent with me, Ms Matthews. You've given me a very difficult time ever since you were elected spokesperson for the nurses." His words were mild, but Kate could hear the resentment and anger underneath.

"That was certainly not intentional on my part. The reports—"

"Reports! From scatterbrained nurses with nothing better to occupy their time! You'd do well to ignore what you hear about me from now on." His pale face flushed to an unhealthy raspberry shade. "If you know what's good for you, that is."

"Is that a threat, Dr. Nash?" Kate asked quietly.

"A warning. The next time you cross me, it will be a threat. I'm a doctor, Ms Matthews. It took me many years of training to get to where I am today. I don't like being challenged by some dissatisfied nurse who can't accept the fact that she's not capable of being a physician. A couple of years of nursing experience and you think you can..."

Kate stared at him transfixed, as he vented his fury. In one coolly observant corner of her mind, she knew she probably looked like a fish with her mouth gaping wide and her eyes bulging, but she couldn't seem to help it. Nash had taken this moment to lose complete and utter control. It was fascinating to see.

Without considering the consequences, Kate asked the first question that popped into her head. "Do you hate all women, Dr. Nash? Or just nurses?"

Immediately Kate knew she'd made a mistake. Nash took a step toward her, his face livid. Would he dare hit her? she wondered. Surely not, but—

"That's quite enough, Ardon." A glacial voice stopped Nash in his tracks.

"Dr. Kincaid!" Nash's face blanched. "I...you didn't...I'd like to explain—"

"I overheard your conversation. I think that's explanation enough."

Nash's blustery bravado evaporated. "Dr. Kincaid, I—"

"I'll see you in my office, Dr. Nash. Now."

"But I'd like to—"

"I don't care what you'd like, Nash. Wait for me in my office."

"But—"

"Now." It was a command not to be opposed. Deflated, Nash slunk from the room, but not before he darted an evil glance at Kate.

She realized then that she was shaking.

"Are you okay?" Chase's voice had an uncharacteristic wobble in it.

"Fine. He just shook me up a little." Kate's hands skimmed the front of her uniform and she noticed their trembling.

"I believe I owe you an apology."

"You? You're my hero, my knight in shining armor!" Kate joked weakly. Her legs suddenly felt very unsteady. If she didn't sit down, she was going to fall down.

"Hardly a hero." With gentle, professional hands, Chase helped her carefully onto the bed. She liked his touch on her skin and was sorry when he released her. "Instead of simply deciding to monitor the situation and keeping an eye on Dr. Nash, I should have taken you more seriously when you complained about Marlis Owens's troubles with him."

"True," she agreed, "you should have."

"You don't pull any punches, do you?"

"Neither do you."

"Not anymore. Not with Nash, anyway. He's shown me his true colors." Chase looked chagrined. "He had no right to speak to you in that manner."

"What are you going to do?"

"I don't know. Calm down, first thing, so I don't throttle him. I forgot that men could still be so stupid in this day and age." His hands were again on her arms, comforting, reassuring. "Really, you look awfully shaken. Are you all right?"

"It's silly." Kate laughed faintly. "It's just that I hate confrontations."

"I never would have guessed, considering how enthusiastic you seem to be about the ones you have with me."

But that's different. I love you. Kate stared at him in dismay, dumbfounded by her startling realization.

"Kate? You look terrible." As he helped her down from the bed, Kate struggled to resist the temptation to sink into his arms. "Come on, I'll take you home."

"That's not necessary. I'm just overreacting. I'm afraid I didn't sleep much last night," Kate said, as a wave of unaccustomed dizziness overtook her. *I was awake thinking about you.*

"I'm giving you the rest of the day off. You don't look very well."

Much as she hated to admit it, the two long sleepless nights were catching up with her. A nap sounded wonderful. "But what about Nash?"

"Let him stew in his own juices for a while. I'll deal with him when I get back to my office."

No one questioned Kincaid when he filled Kate's post with a nurse from Floor Three, or when he escorted her briskly out the door and into his car. She was grateful for his silence as he drove her quickly home and helped her efficiently up the two flights of stairs to her apartment. Once there, Kate dropped wearily into a chair. "Thanks so much, Chase."

He didn't answer. He was delving into her kitchen cupboard. From the depths of the cabinet, she could hear him say, "Take off your clothes."

"What?"

He turned and gave her a disgusted look. "Put on a nightgown or whatever you want to lie down in. Don't you have any tea bags?"

She would have smiled if she hadn't had to bite her lower lip to stop it from trembling. It had been a long time since anyone had taken care of *her*. "Chase—"

"Doctor's orders," he said gruffly. "There they are." His head emerged from the cupboard. "Now, where's the kettle?"

Wearily Kate left him to his search. She was suddenly, achingly tired. As Chase ransacked the kitchen, Kate did the same to her drawers, looking for a pretty nightgown. No matter how many blue-and-yellow hospital gowns Chase had seen, that wasn't the image of her she wanted him to have.

She settled on an embroidered cotton smock Molly had bought her in Mexico. Kate dropped it over her head and simultaneously let her uniform slither to the floor.

She fell onto the bed, drawing the downy comforter around her. She was nearly asleep when she heard Chase step into her bedroom.

"Good," she heard him murmur. He set a mug of steaming tea next to her bed.

"Thanks," she mumbled, more asleep than awake. She thought again how wonderful it felt to have someone take care of her for a change. Ironically, Nash was the person she had to thank for this pleasant little interlude.

"I'd better be going. I have some things to take care of at the hospital," Chase said softly. He was very close to the bed, Kate noticed through heavy-lidded eyes. She could see the fine weave of his jacket sleeve, and then felt the bed give a bit, as he sat down next to her. "Will you be all right?" He passed an exploratory hand across her forehead.

Kate shifted to her side, snuggling deeper into the pillow, and caught his hand beneath her cheek. His breath touched her forehead with the softness of a whisper—warm, minty, clean. And his lips, dry and soft, grazed the tender concave point of her temple. Kate smiled and curled even deeper into her pillow. What a lovely dream. What a lovely, lovely...

Then he was gone. Her lips turned down in a sleepy pout. How did she used to recall a dream after her alarm clock had awakened her? Because try as she might, her phantasmic man would not return.

SHE'D ALL BUT FORGOTTEN that silly little snatch of slumber the next morning, but that was nothing compared to what Dr. Kincaid seemed to have forgotten.

"Good morning," Kate said softly. He looked so intent on his charts she hated to disturb him.

He glanced up with cold, expressionless eyes. "Good morning."

That was it? That was all? No smile? Nothing? Kate frowned.

"Chase..." she began.

"Are you feeling better today?"

"Yes. Much. Thanks, but..."

His eyes took on a hooded, distant look. "I'd like to keep what happened yesterday as quiet as possible, Nurse Matthews. I'd appreciate if you wouldn't mention the situation between yourself and Dr. Nash."

"No, of course not. I wouldn't dream of it."

"I'd like to visit with you for a moment at noon, if that's possible. In my office." With that he turned away.

Now what in the world was wrong with him? Kate questioned. Still, the morning was too busy to consider it further.

At eleven fifty-seven, Kate made her way to the administration office. As usual, Miss Oberon was typing furiously. She glanced up at Kate, then quickly back to her work. Kate picked up a magazine and sat down. Miss Oberon seemed unusually touchy—no greeting, no smile. Was whatever Kincaid had contagious?

Kate smiled inwardly. Perhaps she could cheer him up. He'd been so kind, so...tender, that for the first time she dared to think that Chase was as attracted to her as she was to him. The thought sustained her while she waited. Kate and Chase—she liked the sound. She liked it a lot.

But, as she quickly discovered when Chase called her into his office, that was not the purpose of this "visit." If he'd been tender last night, he was nothing but tough today.

"Sit down, Ms Matthews," he ordered without turning to look at her.

Surprised at his abrupt formality, Kate dropped into the nearest chair.

When Chase finally turned toward her, Kate stifled the small, shocked sound that rose to her lips. He looked exhausted. His eyes, normally clear and alert, were glazed from lack of sleep, the skin around them thin and puffy.

Before she could comment, he said brusquely, "I'd like to apologize again."

"To me?" Kate squeaked. "What for?"

"For not truly listening to you when you complained about Dr. Nash. I didn't believe there was much substance to your complaints. I'm sorry."

Kate bowed her head. "It's just hard for a man like you to understand someone like Nash."

His lips quirked ever so slightly. "Well, Nash and I have had an, er, conversation. We understand each other now. I don't think the nurses will have any more trouble with him—otherwise, the hospital board will be stepping in as a mediator. Nash has seen that threats and bribery won't work."

Kate nodded gratefully. Just as she began to speak, Chase moved restlessly in his chair. "Well, I guess that's all, then. Thank you for stopping by."

Thank you for stopping by? Kate stared at him. What about yesterday? What about . . . ?

"If you'll excuse me, I have some phone calls to make." She was dismissed.

Kate wandered into the hallway brushing her hands across her eyes. She'd seen it, but she couldn't believe it. Kincaid had become as aloof and chilly as those first tense days after he'd learned about the letters she and Nathan had exchanged. What had gone wrong?

She asked herself that question a hundred times in the next few days, but no answer ever suggested itself. Only Molly's antics kept her from dwelling too much on the sudden, radical change in Chase's attitude toward her.

"HE'S COMING, Kate! Can you believe it?"

"I believe it, I believe it." Kate stirred a pot of chili in Molly's kitchen and watched her beaming friend do a joyful little jig. She found it difficult to show much enthusiasm, but Molly had enough for both of them.

"He's such a hunk, Kate. I can't believe it. Can you?"

"I believe it, I be—"

"I know, I know. Don't be so depressed, Kate. Just because Kincaid is a big disappointment in the romance department doesn't mean it's the end of the world. He's always been too stiff and formal for my taste, anyway. Now, Tony Mallenta, there's the guy for me!"

Tony, the male nurse with whom Molly had been corresponding, was coming to visit. Molly would have the opportunity to see firsthand those impressive muscles he'd been photo-documenting for her.

"What should we do? Where should we go? I bought a new dress and I even ordered shoes." Molly snapped her fingers. "I didn't pick up my mail when we came in. Maybe they've arrived. Brother, am I losing it!" She headed for the front door of her apartment.

Kate sat wearily down at the battered kitchen table. At least Molly had something to be happy about, she mused. Unlike Kate, she hadn't been subjected to a week's worth of icy expressions and clipped words. Chase was as cold and distant as the Antarctic these days, and Kate had no idea why.

"Eeeek!"

Kate jumped to her feet. What had Molly seen now? A mouse?

"Katie, this can't be! It just can't be!" Molly came barreling into the kitchen waving a letter. "I just won't let it be!"

"What? What's going on?"

"It's Jerry. He's coming. Some sort of pharmacy thing at the college. But he can't." Molly's eyes were round and terrified. "Can he?"

"It's a free country. Why don't you want him to come? You've been writing to both Tony and Jerry for weeks now."

Molly nodded woodenly.

"Why shouldn't they come to meet you in person?"

"On the same weekend?" Molly wailed. "They're both arriving on Friday night!"

Kate's eyes opened wide. Her lips twitched and she could feel a bubble of laughter building inside. "This weekend?"

Molly groaned.

"Both of them?"

Molly whimpered.

"Where are you going to have them stay?"

Molly swung on her with helpless fury. "Stay? Nowhere! They can't stay. Neither one of them. I can't have them here—not at the same time!"

"Then get in touch with Jerry and tell him that."

"I can't. He's already gone on vacation. He's driving cross-country to get here by Friday."

"So tell Tony that something's come up."

"He's in Wisconsin, visiting his mother. He's going to drive to Fargo on Friday."

"Then call his mother and tell him—"

"His mother is remarried and I don't know her name!" Molly uttered a heart-wrenching sound and collapsed into a chair. "I'm sunk!"

"Just explain to them what happened," Kate suggested, secretly amused to see Molly squirm for a change. "They should understand."

Molly gave her a dirty look. "Would *you* understand?"

Kate remembered Nathan's pirated letters. "No. Not easily."

Molly groaned and fell backward in her chair. "Then I'll just have to leave. You can meet them and tell them I was called out of town."

"No way."

"But you're my best friend!"

"Where were you when I had to face the music with Dr. Kincaid about those letters? Hiding in a storage closet, probably. No deal, Molly. You're on your own."

"But Kate!"

"Didn't you tell Tony and Jerry that you were writing to other men?"

Molly's face crumpled. "No. I never thought . . . I mean, who would have imagined . . . I guess I thought it didn't matter."

"Well then, I guess we'd better get this apartment cleaned up. And bake a few things, too." She threw Molly a sly glance. "To serve to your guests."

"I won't have guests! I'll just leave. Tell them somebody died, an elderly aunt or something."

"Not nice, Molly. You'll lose both of them."

"I will anyway. How can I entertain two guys at the same time?"

"In shifts?" Kate asked facetiously.

Suddenly Molly brightened. "Good idea! I'll bet I could work it out. Breakfast with Jerry, lunch with Tony while Jerry's at his meeting, dinner with . . ." Molly frowned. "That's going to be tough. Maybe I'll have to eat two dinners."

Kate watched her friend, dumbfounded. Molly was actually going to try it!

"Let's see now," Molly muttered, as she bent over a piece of paper. "If I schedule everything just right, I should be able to keep them both happy. With luck, one's a night owl and the other . . ."

Kate just shook her head. Only Molly would even consider such a scheme. Before she had time to arrive at a more realistic suggestion, the telephone rang.

"Get that, will you?" Molly asked. "I'm busy."

Kate rolled her eyes and picked up the receiver. "Molly's place, Kate speaking."

"Kate? I hoped you'd be there."

"John?" She recognized John Hanson, a nurse at St. Mike's.

"Yes. I'm on duty tonight. Floor Three. Several of the nurses have called in sick. Could you or Molly come and fill in?"

Kate glanced at Molly, scribbling away on her notepad. "I'll come. Molly's got her hands full."

"Great. See you soon."

Half an hour later, Kate hurried into the hospital and went straight to the third floor. "Hi. Where do you want me tonight?" she said to John.

"We're really short in the emergency room."

"I'm on my way."

Being in the emergency room again was a real challenge, Kate thought as she reoriented herself. Everything happened so much more quickly there. There was so much drama compared with the steady care that the patients upstairs required.

"Here we go, Kate. Are you ready?" Wanda Kohman, the ER supervisor, asked. "They're bringing in a car-pedestrian accident victim. Child."

Kate nodded and moved toward the entry used by the ambulances. With the flurry of activity around the open doors of the vehicle, she didn't realize for a moment that she knew the victim.

It was Emily Kincaid.

CHAPTER NINE

"EMILY?" KATE MURMURED GENTLY as the child lay on the white examining table, limp as a rag doll. The little girl's eyes flickered open. She was deathly pale except for the large and vivid bruise on her forehead.

"Kate?"

"Don't talk, honey. I'm right here. I'll be with you while the doctor examines you."

"Lucky kid," someone was saying. "Witness says she rolled right under the car between the tires."

Kate gave a silent prayer of thanks. It would kill Chase if Emily were... She shook herself. Emily was all she could think about right now. Someone else would have to handle Chase.

"We'll have to call her father," Kate said in a low voice.

"You know this child?" the physician on duty asked.

"This is Dr. Kincaid's daughter, Emily."

The doctor's lips pressed into a grim line. As Kate shifted closer to the table Emily reached out a hand to her. "Stay with me?"

Kate nodded and smiled reassuringly. She'd already realized that the child was more frightened than hurt. In fact, Emily was almost smiling when Chase ran into the emergency room. Kate moved aside so he could see his daughter.

"Daddy?" Emily's voice sounded weak and thin. "I think I forgot to look both ways."

Kate heard the sob that caught in his throat. "Oh, Em."

He bent over the table, studying her with both his eyes and his hands. As she watched, Kate's heart went out to him. Whatever had made him reject her so quickly and completely didn't matter now. Emily was all that mattered.

"Here are the X rays, if you'd like to look at them," the doctor on duty told him. "No breaks—nothing shows up. A witness said she rolled under the car, but the wheels didn't touch her. I thought we'd keep her for observation tonight and—"

"I'll take her home." Although his voice was strained, Chase's words were authoritative. "I'll stay up and watch her." No one argued.

Kate laid a hand on his arm. It seemed odd to see Chase at the hospital in something other than a suit. He was wearing a short-sleeved polo shirt that exposed the golden tan of his arms. She could feel the soft silky hairs on his forearm.

"If you'd like, I can help you with her. Molly can come in and finish my shift."

He stared at her for a long moment, as if he were deciphering what she'd said. Finally he nodded. "Thank you."

By the time they reached the Kincaid house, Emily's pallor was receding. Two high points of color marked her cheeks and the pink had returned to her lips.

She chattered as Kate helped her into a pair of cotton pajamas sprigged with rosebuds. "I was really scared. I thought I was going to get hurt and that Daddy would be mad at me."

"Honey, how could he be mad at you for having an accident?" Kate asked, marveling at the convoluted logic of children. Just then Chase came through the door carrying a wicker tray filled with tall parfait glasses.

"There's a strawberry sundae with whipped cream and nuts. There's a cherry sundae with double topping. There's a hot fudge sundae with extra fudge. Which one do you want, Em?"

Emily beamed. "Strawberry. No, cherry." Her brow furrowed. "Of course, hot fudge is awfully good...."

Once Emily was settled in bed with her cherry sundae, a dozen comic books, a color TV and her brother at her side, Kate followed Chase into the hallway.

"She's fine, you know."

He nodded. "In my head, I know that. But I keep thinking that she could have been..." His voice turned ragged.

"But she wasn't. She's fine." Kate put her hand on his arm and felt the rock-hard press of his muscles beneath her palm. "You've got to pull yourself together. You're so tense you're going to explode."

A humorless smile twisted his lips. "Isn't that the way? Doctors are always saying things like that to a patient's family."

"Now you know how little good it does."

"I'd like to have thought I was more comforting but—" he shook his head "—there aren't any words to cover this. I'm not as good a physician as I thought, or I would have realized that before now."

"Quit it, Chase," Kate snapped. His head came up and he stared at her, eyes narrowed. "You're punishing yourself for something that wasn't your fault. Emily's fine. Three days from now, she'll hardly remember to tell people what happened and you'll still be feeling guilty that you weren't there to help her cross the street."

With a sudden curse, Chase announced, "I've got to call Amy."

As he moved toward the telephone, Kate tactfully announced, "I'm going to see how that cherry sundae is doing."

He didn't answer. Instead he looked grimly at the telephone, rubbing the palm of one hand against his forehead.

He was still on the phone when Kate returned to the room. Discreetly she stayed in the shadows.

"But she's fine, Amy. Really.... I know doctors can make mistakes. You certainly don't have to remind me of that, but none were made this time. I looked at the X rays myself. She's eating an ice-cream sundae and..."

Storm clouds were brewing on his face. "Of course it's okay if she eats! What do you want me to do, starve her?"

He paused, then, "That's not necessary, Amy. Really. You don't have to..."

Chase grimaced as he caught Kate's gaze. "I suppose, if you insist.... Tomorrow, then, Goodbye."

He dropped the receiver carelessly into the cradle and turned toward her. Kate saw the weary lines etched around his eyes, his sagging posture, his worried frown. It took all her willpower not to go to him and try to soothe away the furrows creasing his forehead. Instead she stood where she was, several feet away, and asked, "Well?"

"She's coming here." He flopped heavily onto the couch, heedless of the springs and cushions, which shuddered beneath him. "She wants to see for herself that Emily's okay."

"That's not unreasonable."

"I suppose not, but I was hoping to avoid it. When things are finished, over and done with, they should be left that way. Healing wounds shouldn't be scratched open." He stared unseeingly over her shoulder at some invisible point on the wall. "That can cause infections and make things worse than they already are."

Make things worse than they already are.

Kate stared at him. Several buttons on his shirt were open, exposing the soft golden hair on his chest. He'd thrown his head back against the cushions of the couch and closed his eyes. His long legs were stretched out before him, crossed at the ankles.

Chase loves Amy. It was like the graffiti scratched on school-yard walls. *Chase loves Amy.* But there was more, she realized. There was another phrase that might be added to that graffiti wall. *Kate loves Chase.*

SHE STAYED WITH EMILY until nearly two in the morning. Nathan had gone to bed at eleven and Kate hadn't bothered Chase, who'd fallen into a fitful sleep on the couch.

Emily had finished her sundae, two comic books and a television show simultaneously, then curled up cozily in her bed. She'd been sleeping for several hours—natural, restful sleep.

It was a good thing she'd been here, Kate thought, considering that Emily's other nurse was fast asleep on the couch. She moved silently from the bedroom into the hall, leaving the door open so that she could hear Emily if she stirred.

From the landing on the staircase, Kate looked down into the living room. A single, low-wattage light illuminated the room, casting a bright circle just beneath its shade and leaving the rest of the room in shadow. Chase had shifted so that one leg was draped over the edge of the couch. He'd thrown his arm across his eyes to protect them from the light of the lamp. His free hand was splayed wide over his stomach, which rose and fell with each breath.

Kate moved silently down the stairs. He was going to have a terribly stiff back if he slept like that. If she could just lift his other leg onto the couch...

He jumped when she touched him. His feet hit the floor and his eyes were wide and clear. "Emily—"

"Emily's fine," Kate soothed. "I was just trying to make you more comfortable. I never dreamed you'd wake up so easily."

"Hospital internship training," he murmured, dropping back to the couch.

"You have wonderful reflexes, that's all I can say." Kate sank onto the couch, too, staying at the far end.

"What time is it?"

"Two."

"I slept that long? Fine night nurse I am." He stretched lazily, his arms high above his head.

Kate grinned. "Maybe if I prove to you just how efficient we nurses are, you'll go before the board and demand a salary hike for us."

Chase groaned, and she held up her hands in mock surrender. "Okay, I'll stop, but just for now. Look out during salary negotiations." Her smile faded. "Really, Chase, I'm sorry all this is happening to you."

"Maybe I'd better go and check on Emily." He started to get up from the couch.

"I just left her. She's sleeping beautifully. Her door is open so we can hear her."

He studied Kate closely. The variegated golds and greens in his eyes flickered mysteriously in the lamplight. "Thank you."

"You're welcome." Kate fought the airy feeling in the pit of her stomach. How did just two innocent words from him make her feel as though she'd just come off a roller coaster?

Kate slipped her hands under her thighs and sat on them. It was either that or reach out to trace the ridge of his cheekbone down to the deep, masculine slash—too manly to be called a dimple—on his cheek.

None of the aloofness or icy hauteur that had been present in him all week was obvious tonight. Kate wondered anew what had made him withdraw so utterly and what had changed him tonight.

As though he'd read her mind, Chase spoke. "I think I owe you an apology."

"Oh?" Kate kicked off her white hospital shoes and tucked her legs beneath her. "For what?"

As he half turned toward her, she unconsciously inched closer. "For my attitude these past few days."

Kate remained silent.

"You aren't going to make this easy for me, are you?" He glanced at her, and she could read the naked discomfort in his eyes.

It was impossible, she decided, to say a single word without revealing the strength of her emotions.

Then, instead of telling her what was on his mind, he changed the subject entirely. "You were wonderful with Emily tonight."

"That's easy. She's a wonderful kid."

He swallowed. "And to think I could have lost her..." Kate saw him shudder.

She was surprised to feel him lift his arm, then rest it on the back of the couch—and around her. The single table lamp bathed them in a soft circle of light. Impulsively she raised her palm to his cheek. "It's over—everything's fine now. Don't think back, Chase. Just look ahead."

"At the moment I don't want to do that, either."

"Then just be in the present. Yesterday's over. Tomorrow isn't here yet. There's only now."

There's only now. The grandfather clock in the hallway chimed the half hour. Two-thirty a.m. A nothing sort of hour, an hour in which the world slept.

It was as though she and Chase were alone in the universe, in a sea of silence. The navy couch was their raft, the circle of light in which they sat their only illumination in a dark world. Kate felt a giddy joy that grew stronger and surer when his arm tightened around her.

"Are you going to stay?" For a moment she thought he would add, "with me."

"I'll stay—for now."

The corners of his mouth lifted into a smile as he lowered his head to hers. Kate's lips parted ever so slightly in delicious anticipation.

He tasted them hungrily, as if they were sweet with honey or fine wine, and she met him fully, kiss for kiss, embrace for embrace, until the silence was broken with the sound of ragged breathing and the calling of each other's names.

Gently Chase pushed her toward the back of the couch, his body pressing hard against her own. Then, with a sharp epithet, a shudder and a quick, rough movement, pulled her up again to a sitting position. His breath was coming in jagged bursts now and his hazel eyes were wide.

"I'm sorry." His voice was harsh, the apology abrupt.

Kate smoothed a trembling hand across her skirt as disappointment flooded through her. She tried to smile. "So am I. Why did you stop?" The joke fell flat.

"I told you earlier that I needed to apologize. Now it's doubly true. My behavior toward you this week has been deplorable."

"I think you'd better explain." With shaking fingers Kate refastened the top buttons of her now crumpled uniform.

He gave a wry laugh and shifted uncomfortably on the couch. Kate longed for the strong warmth of his body next to hers. "What I'd intended to apologize for was my unfriendly behavior at the hospital this past week."

"I wondered what had happened," Kate admitted softly.

"It all started the day you and Nash exchanged words," he said, and Kate nodded.

"You'd fallen asleep that afternoon, just before I left." She nodded again.

"I'm sure you don't remember, but I came and sat on the bed beside you for a few moments..."

So it hadn't been a dream!

"...and I kissed you."

She was about to speak, but he held up his hand. "Don't talk, not yet. I want to explain how I felt afterward." He wove his fingers together behind his head and stared out the night-blackened window. "What I did was hardly appropriate, for one thing. You'd just come away from an unpleasant experience with one doctor. You were obviously exhausted. You didn't need another plying his bedside manner on you." He paused to study her face. "Besides, I didn't like the way you made me feel. I never thought I'd feel those emotions again. I thought all that died when Amy left."

A flicker of hope ignited in her chest.

"I wanted those emotions to stay dormant. I didn't want to like you, Kate. Or anyone, for that matter. I'd loved once and been hurt by it. My life would be so much easier if it were just me, the kids, my profession. No entanglements. No complications."

So that's what Kate was. A complication.

"Because of her immaturity, Amy offered me enough of those. And enough pain."

"So you withdrew?"

He looked at her, surprised, as if the idea had occurred to him for the very first time. "Yes, I suppose I did."

"And you hid behind that icy exterior of yours that makes the North Pole seem like a balmy beach?"

"I was that bad?" His smile was regretful.

"Worse. I didn't know why you were suddenly like that, whether I'd done something—" She paused to swallow the lump of emotion in her throat. "After you'd been so wonderful, I couldn't understand..."

He shifted his weight so that more of Kate's body rested against his. She relaxed in the warmth of his arms, listening to the steady beat of his heart. Her eyes closed with a blissful shudder.

He burrowed his nose in her hair. "I'm sorry for hurting you, Kate. You have this crazy, unpredictable effect on me. I want to stay away but..." She heard a low, pleased growl in his throat and then, "Mmm. Smells like flowers."

She vowed never again to buy another brand of shampoo.

He made a trail of tiny kisses down the side of her face, past her ear, along her jaw, down her neck.

"Mmm. More flowers."

She would wear that fragrance for the rest of her life if it meant hocking her car to pay for it.

She gasped as he flicked his tongue at the corner of her lip.

"Good. No lipstick."

Just as Kate was about to make a third vow, this one to cast out all her cosmetics, a sound niggled at the edge of her consciousness.

Chase heard it the same moment she did. It was Emily at the top of the stairs.

They untangled quickly but clumsily—like a slapstick vaudeville team rehearsing a new act. Kate's disappointment at the interruption was quickly replaced by her concern for Emily.

Chase mounted the stairs three at a time and she was right behind.

"Daddy, I *hurt.*"

"It's no wonder, sweetheart. You got a bad roughing up today." Chase guided the child gently toward her room.

"But I hurt places that I've never even *felt* before."

"Now you know how I felt after you and Nathan made me go horseback riding for four hours."

"I'm sorry," Emily wailed, obviously too uncomfortable to tolerate her father's bad jokes.

While he talked Kate could see Chase running his hands over Emily's bruises, carefully assuring himself that she was all right. Tenderly he tucked his daughter into bed. She quieted as the analgesic he gave her for the pain began to take effect, and Kate stroked her back much as she would soothe a distressed kitten.

He sprawled across the chair next to the bed.

"I guess it's my turn." His eyes crinkled up with a smile. "After all, I had a nap and, uh, whatever that was on the couch."

Kate grinned. "Then I'll leave you two. I doubt I'd be able to pry you away from Emily's side again—even if I wanted to. Sleep sounds good to me, too." She paused in the doorway. "I'm off tomorrow. Does anyone in this household need a good nurse?"

"If you wouldn't mind..."

"Mind? Taking care of one of my favorite people? Anyway, you're going to need a few hours' sleep by then."

A grimness settled about Chase's features. "I certainly will. Amy's arriving tomorrow."

The statement was strangely ominous. Kate had a suspicion that the arrival of Chase's ex-wife was going to have a profound effect—on all of them.

CHAPTER TEN

KATE HURRIED TO THE DOOR at the first sound of the bell. Chase was asleep, weary from his night's vigil with Emily, and Nathan was too involved in a game of Hearts with his sister to even hear the faint chime. She pulled open the door to find a sleek, well-dressed and undeniably beautiful woman on the other side.

"Well?" were the woman's first words. "Aren't you going to let me in?"

"Oh, of course. I'm sorry," Kate murmured, immediately flustered by this unexpected hostility. She felt a blush creep into her cheeks.

The woman strolled past as though Kate were a newel post on the stair railing. Her eyes took in the entire first level, or as much of it as could be seen from the door, before she turned to Kate and asked, "Who are you?"

"I'm Kate Matthews." Kate nervously smoothed the front of her dress. "I'm a nurse—"

"At least Chase had the sense to hire a nurse for Emily. Where is she? I want to see my daughter." The woman paused at the bottom of the stairs. "No, perhaps I'd better talk to Chase first."

"He's sleeping. I can go and—"

"Sleeping? Now? When Emily's been in an accident?" Amy angrily threw her clutch purse against the couch. "Where is that man's mind?" She gave Kate a searing glance. "Don't bother to answer that. I know where Chase's mind is. Same place it's always been. With his patients at the hospital. He should have left Emily there—at least that way she'd get some of her father's attention."

Kate, too dumbfounded by the tirade to speak, stood with her jaw slack and her hands limp at her sides. Could she and this woman be talking about the same person?

"Amy?" He was on the stair landing, barefoot and shirtless and in faded, though obviously expensive, jeans.

"Well, look at you!" Amy began. "You've stopped sleeping in a suit, I see. What do your patients say when you zoom to the hospital looking like Tarzan?"

He padded quietly down the stairs. "I'm taking a few days off. Just until Emily's feeling better." His voice was level.

Kate backed against a wall, feeling very much out of place.

"That won't be necessary, Chase." Amy pivoted on one sharply spiked heel and made her way to the couch. "Emily will be coming home with me."

"What?"

"You're obviously not taking care of her, Chase. Otherwise this wouldn't have happened. I want my daughter with me. Where she's safe."

Chase looked as though he'd been hit in the chest with a two-by-four. The color drained from his face. "You have no right—"

"I have every right, Chase. The child was hit by a car while she was supposedly under your care. What judge or social worker is going to consider that a normal, everyday activity?" Amy gave him a cool, appraising look. "I should have expected it, of course. Some tragedy was bound to occur."

"And what is that supposed to mean?"

Kate closed her eyes and wished herself a million miles away.

Amy didn't even glance Kate's way, obviously accustomed to fighting in front of the "hired help" with her ex-husband. "You've always cared for your profession more than you've cared for your family, Chase. Who always came first in your life? Me?" A hurt, bitter laughter spilled out. "That lasted about six weeks after the honeymoon. Once you'd had enough sex—or whatever it was you married me for—you went right back to the hospital and your patients. Things didn't change very much after the children were born, either, did they? A novelty for six weeks, a nuisance after that."

"I had to return to work sometime, Amy. You do realize I took off a good deal more time than most fathers—"

"You could afford it," Amy insisted hotly.

"Right now isn't the time for this, Amy," Chase warned calmly. "Kate is here, and Emily and Nathan are upstairs. I won't argue with you."

But the more he refused to argue, the angrier Amy became. It was like pouring gasoline on a fire to put it out.

Kate backed toward the door. "Don't worry," Amy was saying. "You don't have to talk to me at all if you don't want. Our lawyers can do the talking for us."

"Lawyers?" Chase repeated. "But the divorce was final before I left Chicago!"

"I made a mistake then. I allowed you shared custody. That was an error, and it could have killed my daughter. I think the custody rights need to be changed—soon."

Kate stuffed her fist into her mouth to suppress the gasp that bubbled up. No shared custody? How could Amy even consider it?

Chase's voice grew still calmer as he recognized the explosiveness of the situation and the state Amy had managed to work herself into.

As unobtrusively as she could, Kate inched closer to the door. No wonder Chase hadn't gone rushing into another relationship—not on the heels of this one.

"Don't patronize me, Chase," she heard Amy say. "And don't think I won't let the authorities know the truth about you! You love your profession better than you've ever loved your family. Our daughter could have been killed yesterday." Amy's voice was shrill, on the verge of hysteria, as she paced the room.

Kate was glad for the rapping of Amy's high heels, which masked the sound of her opening and closing the screen door.

"TONY'S COMING Friday night and Jerry doesn't get in until Saturday morning. That means that if I keep Tony out late enough, he'll sleep in on Saturday and I can spend some time with Jerry. Then, if I plan lunch with Jerry, I can have a late lunch with Tony and spend the afternoon with him. If Jerry and I have an early supper, Tony and I could eat at nine. Then I could beg off, saying I'm tired, and go dancing with Jerry. How does that sound?"

"Like you'll gain weight and wear yourself out all in one weekend," Kate told Molly crossly. Molly had been babbling about her "schedule" for nearly an hour now, and it sounded impossible.

"What's your problem, anyway?" Molly demanded. "I'm the one with the problem!"

Kate couldn't forget that dreadful conversation at Chase's and the confusing, frightening parting shot Amy had aimed at him.

"Katherine Ingrid Matthews! Are you listening to me?"

"Sorry, Molly." Kate leaned heavily against the counter of the nurses' station. "I've got something on my mind tonight. I can't help you with your schedule for the weekend.

Why don't you just introduce them to each other and go out as a threesome?"

"Terrific suggestion, Kate. Just terrific." Molly scraped her chair closer to her friend's. "Why don't you tell me what's bothering you? Maybe that will help."

Kate shook her head. Nothing could help. Nothing but an assurance that Amy's return was not going to wreak havoc with the newly blossoming feelings between her and Chase.

"Well, then," Molly announced, "if you aren't going to help me, I guess I'll go back to work. Maybe you'll be more sympathetic at noon. I certainly hope so." As Molly stormed down the corridor, Kate could hear her muttering, "I could tell Tony I have a sick sister that I'm checking on. And if I do the same with Jerry..."

Kate threw down her pen in frustration.

"You're feeling as good as I am, I see."

She glanced up guiltily. "Chase! You startled me!"

He looked dreadful. His eyes were heavy-lidded from lack of sleep, and the indentations that bracketed each side of his mouth were more deeply etched than usual. His shoulders were rounded as if burdened with the weight of the world.

"We need to talk."

Kate nodded in agreement.

"Morgan's Landing on University Drive. Right after work. Corner table."

She nodded again and he was gone.

Kate kneaded her fingers in her lap. A few days ago, a command performance like this from Kincaid would have sent her heart soaring, but not today. Today she was terrified of what he might say.

MORGAN'S LANDING was dark and dusky with smoke. Kate blinked rapidly as her eyes adjusted to the dimness. Blinded by moving from bright sun into this murky interior, she stumbled a bit, her hand finding a brass rail to balance her.

"Table, miss?"

"I'm here to meet someone. Doctor—"

"Right this way, please. Watch your step."

She followed the waiter's white-shirted back to a table in the darkest recess of the pub. Chase's face was illuminated only by a thick, stubby candle in a yellow, bubble-glass vase. Even in the candlelight, she could see the tension in his face.

"What are we doing? Hiding out?" she joked as she sank into a leather barrel chair, but the flicker in his eyes showed that the humor was lost on him.

His elbows were leaning on the table, and his hands circled a perspiring glass filled with ice and what looked like scotch.

"A drink for you?"

Kate glanced at the waiter. "Soda with a twist of lime, please."

Chase took a swig of whatever was in his glass and shuddered. "It's no wonder this stuff destroys your liver," he muttered. "It'd eat through cast iron."

"Why do you drink it then?"

"I don't—usually."

Kate weighed her words before speaking. "Is it Amy?"

A grim expression contorted his features. "It's always Amy."

Her heart plummeted. Why had Amy Kincaid chosen now to come? The waiter had returned, bringing her drink, and Kate toyed with the slice of lime in her glass. She waited silently.

"Every time I think I have things resolved, something happens to create chaos again." He stared intensely into the bottom of his glass. "It's worse this time, because Emily's involved. At least Amy decided against taking Emily away immediately."

"But you had nothing to do with her accident!"

"She's staying with me. Isn't that enough?"

"No, it isn't." Kate gathered her courage. "I heard the two of you yesterday. You were fighting about more than Emily's well-being. Anyone could tell that."

"I suppose you're right." A weary smile tugged at his lips. "Amy's volatile at best. I like peace and quiet. Together we're like a chemistry experiment gone wrong."

They were both silent for some minutes. Kate could hear a clock ticking, a big Seth Thomas on the wall behind her. Helplessly she said, "You're too hard on yourself," wishing she had a solution to offer him.

"Am I?" His eyes were glazed in pain. "What if I lose custody of Nathan and Emily?"

"She couldn't have been serious!" Kate exclaimed. "Could she?"

He nodded. "Amy's very unhappy right now. Her second marriage isn't working out. All she has are the children. I have no doubt that Amy loves our children," he said with quiet seriousness, "but that doesn't make her above using them to hurt me. Maturity is not Amy's strong point."

He stared off into the dusky blackness of the small room. "She's so angry at men in general right now, I suppose it seems only logical to hurt whichever one is most vulnerable. If her second husband is oblivious to her unhappiness, well, then..."

A cold rock formed in Kate's stomach. "Is she getting divorced?"

"Looks that way. The ironic thing is that she even told me she realizes now I wasn't such a terrible husband, after all." He gave a dry chuckle. "Once Amy's single again, then what?" He spoke pensively, more to himself than to Kate.

Yes, then what? thought Kate. Hadn't Amy kept his letters? Perhaps she'd saved some of her heart for him, too.

The atmosphere of Morgan's Landing suddenly seemed thick and cloying as she asked the question that burned on her lips. "Do you know the answer, Chase?"

He lifted his head, and in the dimness, the expression in his eyes was indiscernible. He snapped a swizzle stick in two with a sharp crack. "I've never, ever, tried to second-guess Amy." He stared at the broken plastic in surprise, as if he hadn't realized it was he who had broken it. "She's a very complex woman."

He seemed to forget for a moment that Kate was there. When he spoke again, he sounded almost hesitant, his voice so soft she could barely hear it. "Maybe I misjudged Amy. Or judged her too harshly." Then he glanced up and smiled faintly at Kate. "I doubt it, though, knowing Amy."

Was he regretting the rift between them?

"Amy and I always had dreadful fights. She was incapable of not saying exactly what was on her mind. When we fought she always reminded me very much of a spoiled child. I imagine her second husband wasn't so tolerant of her... outspoken nature."

Amy was free again. Kate's eyes skimmed the rugged, handsome planes of this man's face. The man she loved. Masculine, charming, kind. What more could a woman want? Amy had admitted she'd given up more than she'd first realized. Now that she was single again, would Amy want her husband back?

Chase uttered a sound that was half expletive and half sigh. "Our priorities were different. I had my work and my family. Amy wanted a glittering social life, too. After a day of work and an evening with the children, I had no time for climbing some slippery social ladder." He propped his elbows on the table again and wearily leaned his forehead against the palms of his hands.

"Amy's immature obsession with being and having the biggest, the best, the newest, wore me out. She wanted everything life had to offer, but she had no appreciation for my work. Only the paycheck it earned." He raised his head to give Kate a tired smile. "Keeping Amy happy was a little bit like capturing moonbeams—impossible, but intriguing nevertheless."

It took a long time for Kate to form her next words. "Chase, do you still love her?"

It took him even longer to answer.

"I loved her once," he admitted frankly. "But not with the same...affection I feel for you." Gently he brushed a stray lock of hair from Kate's cheek and his fingertips lingered lightly on her skin. "I'm just beginning to realize that kind of love exists."

Kate's heart gave a little jolt. *That kind of love...*

"I thought perhaps you still loved Amy." She hurried on when she saw the question in his eyes. "You've never said a really unkind word about her. You're so patient with her—even when she tries to hurt you."

His face clouded. "She's the mother of my children, Kate. What kind of man would I be if I ridiculed or mistreated her? Could you love a man like that? A man who'd shared so much with a woman and then turned from her completely?"

Kate hadn't thought of it in quite that way, and a rush of embarrassment engulfed her. How little credit she'd given him!

"No," she said honestly. "When you describe it like that I couldn't. I love so much about you, but I think what I love best is your gentleness and tolerance. You're right. You wouldn't be those things if you treated Amy any differently." Chase smiled in satisfaction and reached for her hand. "I'm sorry I ever doubted you," she added softly.

The emotional tension between them was so overwhelming that Kate felt relieved when Chase diverted her with a gentle, "Enough about Amy. How are you? Really?"

"Better, now that we've talked." Making an effort to change the subject, she said lightly, withdrawing her hands from his, "The only real excitement I know of is in Molly's life."

"Mulgrew? What's she up to now?" Chase wondered. "Something legal, I hope."

As Kate explained the two visitors and the schedule Molly had devised to keep them apart, Chase's smile grew.

"She thinks she's going to hide them from each other for the entire weekend and not have them suspicious?"

"You know Molly. Nothing seems impossible to her."

"I'd think this would daunt even her."

Kate grinned ruefully. "Actually, I hope she gets caught. Molly deserves it."

Chase smiled. "Oh, I don't know. I might never have learned to know you so well if it weren't for Ms Mulgrew. And Nathan." He reached across the table again to place his hand over her own and as they touched, everything in Kate's world was right once more.

"I CAN'T GO ON, Kate. I just can't." Molly was draped theatrically across Kate's couch, a cold compress on her forehead and a pained expression on her face.

"Of course you can. You have to." Kate wrung out a new cloth and tossed it at her friend. "You have two supper dates tonight. One early, one late. You're going to a play at the community theater and then dancing. I read your schedule."

"I can't!" Molly wailed. "I've already eaten two breakfasts and two lunches and told so many lies that if I were Pinocchio my nose would have grown all the way to Minneapolis. I'm exhausted."

"Then introduce Tony and Jerry to each other and explain what happened."

"No!"

"Then get up. You have to get ready for dinner." Kate tugged on Molly's hand. "Neither of them can find you here."

"But that's why I came here," Molly pointed out. "I'm hiding."

"Out!" Kate pointed toward the door. "Now."

"Some friend you are."

"Right. I'm a great friend. And an advocate of honesty."

"Honesty is the worst policy," Molly insisted.

"Honesty is the best policy," Kate corrected. "And until you tell those guys the truth, you'll get no sympathy from me."

"Sadist," Molly muttered as she trailed out of the apartment. "And I always thought you were such a nice person."

Kate smiled and closed the door behind her friend. This was good for Molly, she told herself. Good in the same way discipline is good for children. And Molly Mulgrew was due for a lot of discipline.

CHAPTER ELEVEN

"PLEASE HELP US, Kate. You've got such good ideas. Please?"

"I don't know, Emily. I'm not sure this is a good time to—"

"Just help us plan a birthday party for Dad. And maybe you could help us get his present. Nathan and I have a great idea for a gift, but we don't know how to get it."

"Oh, I suppose," Kate relented, giving the wide-eyed girl a smile. "Your dad needs a break these days."

A birthday party might cheer him up, Kate mused. Though Amy had returned to Chicago for the time being, she'd been riding him hard about Emily's supervision. In addition, pressures were mounting at the hospital.

The board was pressing for further financial cuts while Chase insisted that they were down to bare-bones essentials already. Worse yet, a face-off between management and labor seemed inevitable. If that happened, she and Chase would find themselves on opposing sides. Now she understood why it was unwise to have a personal relationship with someone in the same workplace; no matter what happened, whether or not the nurses were given larger salaries, her relationship with Chase would suffer.

But Emily and Nathan had no knowledge of the turmoil at work. Their only concern was their father's birthday.

"Come into the living room," said Emily. "We want to tell you about our idea for his present."

Absently Kate followed the pair through the Kincaid house, her mind a million miles away. She decided that a distraction might be just what she needed right now. Still focused on her own problems, she suddenly noticed Nathan looking at her expectantly. "Kate? Don't you think that would be great?" he was asking.

"What? I'm sorry. I didn't hear what you said," Kate apologized.

"A portrait. A painting of the three of us. For over the fireplace. Don't you think Dad would like that? It would fit right here." He pointed to the unadorned wall above the mantel. "Em and I measured."

Kate's eyebrows arched in surprise. A family portrait without their mother?

"We always had one over the mantel in our other house," Nathan explained. "Dad said he missed it, but when he asked Mom if he could have it, she said no. We thought it would be nice to give him a new portrait."

"And since only the three of us live in this house, we thought it would be all right if Mom weren't in this one." Emily's face was bright with anticipation. "We've saved up our money for a long time and we have a good photo of the three of us the painter could use. What do you think, Kate?"

"It's a lovely idea, but a portrait is very expensive and might take more time than you have until your father's birthday. Have you looked into it? And how much do you have saved?"

When they told her, Kate shook her head. "That's a lot of money, I know, but it's not enough to commission a portrait, unless..." The proverbial light bulb went on in her head. "There's a man at the hospital who does beautiful portrait work as a hobby. He's not a professional, but maybe he'd—"

"Ask him, will you Kate? Please? We don't have much time."

"Oh, all right," Kate acquiesced. "You talked me into it."

Chase was so preoccupied these days that she hardly ever saw him. They'd done little more than say hello. The least she could do was help his children get him a birthday present.

The silence from the Kincaid household over the next few days had her wondering if she'd made the right decision. Perhaps his withdrawal meant he didn't want her meddling in his life—or his birthday parties.

By Friday, when the long-silent telephone rang, she'd nearly given up hope of hearing from him. "Hello?"

"Kate?"

"Chase, is that you?"

"Have you forgotten the sound of my voice? It hasn't been that long, has it?"

"Nearly." She struggled to keep the girlish breathlessness from her voice. At her age, she should be over that, she thought, irritated with herself for betraying her emotions.

"I'm sorry. Busy week. Between the hospital board and an increase in my private practice, I haven't had much time."

"I understand." Word was spreading about Chase's skill and compassion with the elderly. Miss Oberon had confided to Kate that his appointment book was already filled for weeks to come. Soon St. Mike's would have to recognize the need for a geriatric wing, if Chase were to continue working at the hospital.

He murmured, "I believe you do." There was a long silence between them before he added, "I checked the schedule. I see you aren't working this weekend."

"No. That means I can sleep in till noon if I want."

"And perhaps you'd be free to have dinner with me this evening."

Kate quickly went through Molly's lecture about playing hard-to-get, then tossed it aside. "Sure. Name a time."

"Tonight at seven all right? It's my birthday tomorrow and the kids seem to want me out of the house tonight. I took an oath to be gone till midnight, go directly upstairs to bed and not look in the living room until tomorrow morning."

The streamers and balloons, Kate thought to herself. The children were so eager to decorate that they were doing it right under their father's nose. There'd be no surprises left for Chase's party except the portrait—if Hank Burns got it finished today.

Of course, there was also the little matter of the surprise she'd arranged for Nathan and Emily. That should keep the party hopping even if the kids did reveal all their schemes to Chase.

AT SEVEN, KATE WAITED ALONE inside the large screened-in porch that all the apartment residents shared. She was gliding back and forth on a green-and-white wicker rocker, her eyes closed, her ears tuned to the wind rustling in the trees.

"You look so peaceful I hate to disturb you." Chase was leaning against the door frame, one leg crossed in front of the other, his hands in his pockets, blond head held to one side. Framed by the doorway, his shoulders nearly filling it with their width, he could have stepped from the pages of *Gentlemen's Quarterly.*

"Wow." Kate clapped her hand over her mouth. "I mean, hello."

The smile lines at the corners of his eyes deepened. "I liked *wow* better."

"Nice suit."

"Thank you. Not too much?"

"Not a bit." Kate couldn't pull her gaze away.

He wore a classic silk double-breasted sport jacket of pale cream and a matching silk dress-shirt. His trousers were a woody tan color, and his tie was of the same wood-hued brown and cream. Even his Italian-made shoes matched perfectly.

"You look better than a double-dip chocolate-almond-fudge ice-cream cone."

"I'm flattered. Especially when the compliment comes from a creamy strawberry-cheesecake confection like yourself."

Kate stood up and whirled around once in her full-skirted strawberry-colored sundress. "Do you think we're talking this way because we're hungry, or do we just have severe food fixations?"

"My fixations don't have anything to do with food," Chase murmured, holding out his arm. "But let's discuss this over dinner."

The car windows were open and Kate threw her head back to allow the gentle breezes to sift through her hair. She didn't care if she ever ate again. Just being with Chase sated her in a way she'd never dreamed possible.

"Is this all right?"

They were parked in front of Andretti's, the newest Italian restaurant in town. "Wonderful. I've been wanting to try the food. Northern Italian, isn't it?"

"So the advertisement says."

Dinner was an elegant affair, including pasta in a delicate cream sauce and artfully grilled fish. They both declined dessert, Kate declaring herself too full "for at least the next two hours," then lingered almost that long over cup after cup of fragrant coffee. On their way out of the restaurant, she gave a contented sigh. "Thank you. The meal was delicious. And so was the company—especially compared to this last week at work."

"You're welcome—I think. Speaking of work, I noticed that Ms Mulgrew has been calling in sick," Chase commented as they walked to the car, his arm lightly around her shoulders.

Kate suppressed a smile. "I think she had a headache."

"Anything caused by her... guests?"

"Molly did manage to keep the men apart until noon on Sunday. Then something went awry and they both came to her doorstep to pick her up."

Chase chuckled. "Then what?"

"She finally did what I'd told her to do all along. She introduced them to each other and explained what had happened."

"And?"

"I was right. Neither of them minded very much. After all, they're on a pretty even footing, both having just met her. In fact, they discovered an intense common interest in baseball."

"So they went to a baseball game as a threesome?"

"No. The Minnesota Twins were on television. Tony and Jerry made themselves at home in front of the TV talking baseball and left Molly to serve snacks from the kitchen."

"Then why is she sick? It doesn't sound as though she suffered much."

"Well, she'd eaten so many meals with the two of them that she decided she needed some exercise," Kate explained. "And neither of them were talking to her, because they spent the commercials rehashing the games. So Molly decided to go to the park and bash a few tennis balls."

"And that's where she got sick?"

"No, that's where she tripped and fell against the corner of a picnic table. Molly's got a black eye."

"She stayed home because of a black eye?"

"And a touch of food poisoning. When she got back to the apartment, the guys had gone for food. They just didn't tell her that they'd forgotten the potato salad in the car for an inning before bringing it into the apartment."

"So she has a black eye *and* food poisoning?"

"Nothing serious. It's really her knee that worries her."

"Her knee?" Chase sounded a little breathless.

"After they left, Molly was so angry with the two of them for ignoring her all afternoon that she kicked her door."

"And hurt her knee?"

"Yes. Then she lost her footing and fell down."

"I see." Chase's lips were trembling with the effort to keep a straight face. "So she has food poisoning, a black eye and an injured knee. Not to mention a headache from all the stress."

Kate finally couldn't suppress her own laughter any longer. "But she's vowed never to tell a lie again."

He threw Kate a quick, amused glance. "I feel as though nothing I can do will compete with Ms Mulgrew's antics."

"Thank goodness," Kate muttered.

"Where's the nearest all-night grocery store?" he surprised her by asking.

"Across from the mall. Why?"

"Never mind. Just trust me." With that, he swung the car onto a side street that led to the shopping center. He pulled into the parking lot in front of a brightly lit grocery store and stopped the car.

"I'll be right back."

Kate watched in amazement as he jumped out of the car and loped toward the building. He was out again in a matter of minutes, carrying a brown paper sack and wearing an odd smile.

"Just what did you buy in there?" she asked curiously.

"You'll have to wait and see."

Instead of turning into Kate's street he headed in the opposite direction.

"And where are you taking me?"

"You'll have to wait and see about that, too."

Finally he turned down a road that told her where he was intending to take them. "Chase! This is the park!"

"I know."

"It's almost midnight! We shouldn't be here now."

"It's a park, and I'm parking," he pointed out logically. He shut off the ignition. "I'll carry the bag. But I have to get something else out of the trunk first."

"But—"

"Head for those big trees. The ones with the wide trunks. I'll catch up."

Kate shrugged her shoulders and stumbled through the thick grass, finally bending down to remove her high-heeled sandals.

"I think we can sit here."

She gasped. She hadn't realized he was that close behind her. She spun around to see him spreading a sleeping bag on the grass near the base of the trees. He opened the zipper to expose the fuzzy flannel interior of the bag.

"There. You should be comfortable sitting on this. Good thing Nathan didn't take it out of the trunk after his camp-out." He dropped onto the bag, leaned back against the tree and stretched his legs. "Join me?"

Dumbfounded, she did.

Then, just when she thought her surprises were complete, he dug into the bag he'd brought from the grocery store. In it were two spoons from the household section and two pints of ice cream.

"Chocolate almond fudge or strawberry cheesecake for you?" he inquired.

It was a moment before Kate managed, "I do love chocolate almond fudge." Never before had her words held such a blatant double meaning.

"And I feel the same way about strawberry cheesecake ice cream." He gave her an odd look. "Seems we're made for each other." Then he lifted a spoonful of ice cream to her lips. "Taste." Automatically she licked it.

"This is wonderful." Kate gave a blissful shudder—the sweetness on her lips, the warm dampness of the night air, the feel of Chase's shoulder next to hers...

"Why are we whispering?"

"It's just so beautiful and so quiet here. I hate to break the spell."

"It won't break unless you want it to."

She stared at him, his features unreadable in the darkness. "Why did you do this?"

"First, a question for you. Do you like it?" His husky voice reverberated in her ears and sent a shiver down her spine.

"I love it. It's so... romantic."

"She was right then."

"What?"

Kate felt Chase put down the ice-cream carton and spoon, then shift closer to her.

"I dated a girl in high school once—Sherry Winston was her name—and she told me that she thought the most romantic thing in the entire world must be eating ice cream under the stars."

"The *most* romantic thing?"

"Keep in mind that we were fifteen at the time." He traced a pattern on her cheek. "It seemed pretty advanced to me. I've never actually tried it until now."

He draped his arm around her shoulders and Kate curled into its warmth.

"You'll have to thank Sherry Winston for me."

She felt his body shake with a low, rumbling laugh. "She's been married four times since I knew her. Apparently Sherry found just about everything romantic."

The warm air caressing her arms made her sigh with pleasure. She curled her toes into the fleece lining of the sleeping bag and simply enjoyed the comfortable silence between them. And all the while, she breathed in Chase's clean, woodsy scent, she longed to explore the strongly defined lines and angles of his face.

Suddenly he leaned toward her and caught the curve of her jaw in his hand, urging her even closer. Kate's eyelids fluttered down as his lips sampled hers.

His mouth was soft and dry and gentle. Kate heard a little sigh in the night air. Hers? Then the tenderness became a more persistent pressure, sweeping her up in the deliciousness of the moment. She moved her arms to the back of his neck and clung to him.

Without drawing his lips from hers he said, "You taste like chocolate almond fudge." Kate giggled at the tickling sensation of his lips vibrating next to hers. Vampishly, she batted her eyelashes so that they quivered against his cheekbone.

"I *love* chocolate almond fudge." With that, he pushed her gently back and Kate found herself in a reclining position.

His hard body pressed against her own left her breathless—literally. "Chase, you're... squashing me."

He rolled to one side. "No give."

"Hmm?"

"The ground has no give. Doesn't work as well as a bed."

The thought made her cheeks flame in the blackness until she wondered if she were visibly on fire.

"Chase..." she began.

"Don't worry," he murmured as he took tiny nibbles at the outer rim of her ear. "There are no inflatable mattresses in the car."

It was difficult to decide if she felt relieved or disappointed as the minute jolts of electricity raced through her nervous system. He'd found the tender spot just below her ear and was worrying it with his tongue. The sensation made Kate's toes curl and little stars, like fireflies flitted before her eyes. She even heard bells ringing.

Not bells, exactly. More like... beepers.

The expletive Chase muttered as he sat up made Kate's eyes widen.

"I didn't know you carried a beeper. Are you on call?" Kate struggled upright and smoothed the rumpled front of her dress.

"I always carry it. But they've got strict instructions not to call unless something's burning, exploding or being blown away."

"Sounds serious."

"I'm afraid it might be. I'm sorry, Kate, but I guess this means our night in the park is over."

"It was lovely." She stroked his cheek and could feel the slight roughness there. "Sherry Winston was right. It is romantic."

He grinned and leaped to his feet. "Come on. I'll take you home on the way to the hospital." As he drew her up, he pulled her close, until the softness of her body was resting along the lean hardness of his. She inhaled sharply. His head came down, and his searching lips quickly, forcefully, met hers.

When he stepped back from her to speak, his voice was satisfyingly ragged and regretful. "I'd better hurry. Come on."

Her heart still pounding like a trip-hammer, Kate helped him roll the sleeping bag and toss it into the trunk. Her pulse had barely returned to normal by the time Chase pulled up in front of her apartment.

"Thanks—for everything," she murmured as she slipped from the car. "And I nearly forgot—happy birthday."

"Thank you. I'm afraid the children are planning something. That always gives me some trepidation."

"I'm invited for cake," Kate told him, knowing full well there was more than a birthday cake involved in tomorrow's festivities.

"Perfect." Then he glanced at his watch. "I'd better go."

Thoughtfully Kate watched until the faint red of the taillights disappeared around a corner. Then she strolled toward the house, her sandals swinging from her finger, her head tipped back to see the stars.

CHAPTER TWELVE

"HAPPY BIRTHDAY!"

Nathan and Emily carried the lovingly made, if somewhat uneven, layer cake into the living room where Chase sat reading the paper. Kate followed behind lugging the large gift-wrapped parcel.

Chase looked up over the top of his reading glasses, and a delighted grin lit his face.

"For me?" He dropped the paper to the floor and, leaning forward, elbows on his knees, studied the crooked and rather garishly iced cake.

He nearly took Kate's breath away. Chase—in ordinary blue jeans and a white polo shirt, sockless and wearing topsiders, his hair carelessly rumpled. She'd never seen anyone handsomer.

"And who baked this?" he asked as he took a swipe of frosting with his index finger.

"I did," Emily said proudly. Then her face fell. "But the layers didn't come out even. Kate said the rack was tipped in the oven and the batter kind of flowed to one side. Nathan thought we could even it out with frosting, but it's still pretty crooked."

He glanced up and Kate could see the laughter in his eyes. "Looks great to me. What's that?" He pointed to the package.

"It's from me and Em, Dad." Nathan took the parcel from Kate and laid it in his father's outstretched arms. "We hope you like it."

She watched him closely as he unwrapped the package. Hank Burns had done a beautiful job of reproducing the photo she'd given him and the children were so excited. He simply had to like it.

He laughed with the children as he tore away the wrapping paper, but the laughter died as he peeled away the cardboard protector and looked at the portrait. He was so suddenly and totally serious that Kate felt a twinge of alarm.

"Dad, do you like it?"

"It's okay, isn't it, Daddy?"

"We thought it could go over the fireplace."

"We know Mom wouldn't let you have our other one and..."

When Chase looked up, Kate glanced away, shocked at the emotion she saw in his eyes.

"It's..." He could hardly speak.

Kate gave herself a mental scolding. Of course he didn't want a family picture *without his wife*; it had to remind him of his failed marriage! Why hadn't she thought of that? It would be like a banner strung across the doorway crying Failure! She was the adult, not Nathan and Emily. She should have stopped it before it got this far....

"It's the nicest gift I've ever received."

Kate glanced at him again. It wasn't anger she'd seen! Not at all!

Emily lunged at her father. "You scared me! You didn't say anything and I thought you hated it."

"I could never hate anything as beautiful as this." His voice was choked with feeling.

"It's okay, isn't it, Dad, that we left Mom off the picture?" Nathan asked. "She doesn't live here, so we figured..."

Kate observed him carefully from beneath her lashes, more eager than the children for his answer.

"It's just fine, Nate. Just fine."

All three of them relaxed at the words.

Before any new emotion could overtake them, Kate announced, "By the way, I have a present, too."

Chase's eyes met hers in a glance as intimate as a caress. "Do I get it now or later?"

"Now." She was embarrassed at the erotic jolt his question engendered—embarrassed and excited.

"Oh." He sounded disappointed.

"Actually, it's a gift for all of you. A birthday and housewarming and welcome-to-Fargo present."

"What is it? Where?"

"Let's see it!"

Kate dashed out to her car and returned carrying a large white box with ventilation holes on the lid. An odd scraping sound issued from within.

Chase raised an eyebrow and held back, but Nathan and Emily dived for the carton and pulled away the cover.

"A puppy! Dad, look, a puppy!" Emily scooped the little dog out of the box and it licked her nose.

"It's a golden retriever and he's three months old," Kate explained, one eye still on Chase, waiting for his reaction. "They're supposed to be wonderful with kids. You've got such a large fenced-in yard that I thought he'd have room to play. But they'll take him back if you don't want him."

"No!" Emily shrieked as Nathan shouted, "No way!"

"Well, Chase," Kate addressed him, "what do *you* say?"

A smile as wide and bright as Emily's broke across his face. "I say he stays."

Before their father could change his mind, Nathan, Emily and the puppy vanished from the living room. "Well, that was quick," Kate commented. "They've already taken off with your birthday present."

Chase stretched and stood up. "Good. I'll use that against them when it's time to clean puddles off the floor."

Kate frowned. "Did I go too far? Maybe you don't want a dog."

Chase rubbed the back of his neck and stretched again. "Actually I've been thinking about getting one. I just haven't had much time for shopping." He reached out and pulled her toward him. Kate melted into his arms, snuggling against the muscular length of his body.

"I'm glad you took today off," she murmured, her hands floating lightly over his rib cage.

"The kids would have been devastated if I hadn't. Anyway—" he gave her a mock-accusing glance "—I'm tired. I didn't get to bed until late last night."

She held up a hand. "Now don't go blaming me! It was your idea to sit in the park until—"

"Yeah, but it certainly wasn't my idea to have the fire-alarm system at the hospital go berserk and scare dozens of people half out of their wits. Took me most of the night to get things straightened out."

Chase ran the tips of his fingers down the outside of her arms, raising goose bumps everywhere he touched. "How about going for a ride?"

"But what about Nathan and Emily?"

"Do you think they'll care if we're here?" Chase looked out the window where the kids were rolling on the grass with the puppy. "I'll tell them we'll be gone for an hour or so. They can entertain themselves."

Neither of them spoke as they drove along the tree-lined streets. They traveled past the grand and sprawling houses in contented silence, until he pulled off onto a side road that led to the river. Then Kate said, "I always like it down here. Nice and peaceful."

"And private." Chase hooked his hand around her shoulder, drawing her closer. "I've been waiting all morning to do this." He leaned forward and captured her mouth with his own.

She could feel the tip of his tongue tracing a delicate pattern on her lips. A purr of delight and pure pleasure escaped her.

Chase pulled back to study her, his index finger tracing the outline of her features. "This is the first time in a lot of years that I've liked my time off better than my time at the hospital."

"Oh? Why?"

"Because I can't do this at the hospital," and he drew her so close that she could feel the steady beating of his heart near hers. "Or this," and he fastened his mouth over hers in a greedy kiss.

"And especially not this—"

"Chase Kincaid!"

He gave her a guilty grin. "You mean I *still* can't do that?"

Kate adjusted her clothing. "Certainly not in public!"

"In private, then?"

"I didn't say that," she hedged.

"Let's go to your place." Chase sat up straight and moved to start the car.

"Molly's there."

His hand fell away from the ignition. "Why? Doesn't she have a place of her own?"

"She's hiding."

"Hiding? Did she rob a bank?" Chase grimaced. "It figures."

"No, silly. It's just that both of her pen pals wrote her a letter saying they'd call today. She thinks one of them might ask for some sort of commitment. They've been pretty competitive since that crazy weekend. Molly isn't sure she's ready for that, so she doesn't want to talk to either of them."

"Why doesn't she just not answer her phone?"

"You don't know Molly. She can't let a phone ring without answering it, and she's too curious to take it off the hook. That's why she called me and asked if she could 'think' in my apartment today."

Chase shook his head. "It doesn't make a bit of sense, but I don't know why Molly Mulgrew should start making sense now." He pounded his fist against the steering wheel. "And I'll be darned if I'm going to check into a motel room with you at eleven-fifteen in the morning. Both our reputations will be shot within hours if what I hear about the grapevine in a town this size is correct."

"You've got that right," Kate agreed cheerfully. "So I think the best thing for you to do is take me home—to yours, not mine. I'll make you some lunch."

"And then I can send the kids shopping for puppy supplies." Chase began to grin.

"That should take at least an hour."

"Two or three if they comparison shop."

They were laughing and holding hands as they mounted the steps to the Kincaid house, but their laughter died quickly.

"Telephone, Dad." Nathan met them at the door, his face pale and grim.

"Something wrong at the hospital?" Chase immediately became all business.

"No. It's Mom."

A heavy feeling of dread settled in Kate's stomach. What did Amy want now? Was she still ranting about Emily's accident and how Chase should be punished for his carelessness? She reached out a hand to Chase, but he was already a step ahead, and her outstretched hand caressed the air.

Kate followed him inside.

"You can't, Amy! It's ridiculous. Absolutely ridiculous. You must be out of your mind...."

Kate tried to tune out the furious words and hurried thankfully to the front of the house when the doorbell rang.

"Dr. Chase Kincaid?"

"He's on the phone right now," Kate explained, wondering who the dark-suited man was.

"I'm off, Kate. Who's . . . ?" Chase's face blackened and he took a step backward, but it was too late. The man lunged forward and placed an envelope in his hand. "Personal service complete at 11:45 a.m. Thank you, Dr. Kincaid." Then he turned and walked back to his car, leaving the dumbfounded pair in the doorway.

"Chase, what is it?"

He stared at the packet in his hands for a moment before he tore open the envelope. "That was a process server."

"What does it mean?" Kate felt fear clutch her heart.

He stared for a long moment at the legal document in his hand. "Amy's just served me with papers claiming I'm an unfit father."

"Unfit? You? But that's crazy!"

"She said she'd do everything in her power to get full custody of the kids."

"She can't do that, can she?"

His face had gone as white as his shirt. Chase stumbled backward and dropped into the closest chair. "She says she's heard through Em and Nathan and a mutual friend on St. Mike's advisory board that I'm 'friendly' and 'intimate' with the nurse who was here to take care of Emily. She's claiming, among other things, that my 'womanizing' is a bad example for the children."

An agonized protest caught in Kate's throat. Could she really be part of the reason Chase might lose his children?

Wearily he continued, "She didn't say it in so many words, but she's eaten with jealousy, Kate."

Kate just stared at him.

"It's killing her to think of her children growing fond of someone else—someone I might be involved with. I suspect part of her jealousy stems from the fact that she resents sharing Emily and Nathan's affection."

"What are we—you—going to do?" Kate knelt down beside his chair.

When he looked up there was a lost, inconsolable look in his eyes. "I don't know. Fight her, I suppose." He sighed and the sound tore at Kate's heart. "I don't want to fight with Amy anymore. I never wanted to fight with her." He scraped his fingers through his hair. "We loved each other once. Nathan and Emily are proof of that. What went wrong?"

Kate jumped to her feet, unable to stop herself. "*Amy went wrong*, Chase," she burst out, her voice sharp with anger. "Can't you see that?" She paced in a small circle, willing herself to be calm. Kate had no doubt that Amy loved her children, but she certainly wasn't above using them against Chase. Amy was going to ruin everything for them. Kate could see it as clearly as she could see Chase's brooding face.

He got slowly, painfully, to his feet and gave her a forced, apologetic grin. "I'd better call my lawyer." Then, as if in afterthought, he turned back to her. "I don't think you and I had better see each other for a while, Kate. Not until this is settled. I don't want to give Amy any more ammunition."

He was right, of course. Their own needs were secondary to those of a father and his children. She watched as he dialed the telephone, a look of grim determination on his face.

Kate stretched out her hand to him and then allowed it to drop to her side. She remembered having this sensation once before—as a tiny child, at the beach. Desperately she'd wanted some of the wonderful beach for herself, but each time she picked it up, the tiny grains of sand slipped through her fingers and were lost. It was like that now. She wanted Chase, she realized, wanted him with a desperation unlike anything she'd ever experienced. And he was slipping through her fingers....

When he was finished on the phone, he didn't speak for several minutes. "I'm going up to my lawyer's office now," he finally said to Kate. "He thinks we should get on this right away."

She nodded mutely.

"And he agrees that you and I shouldn't see each other for a while. He suggested we not speak at the hospital unless it involves a work-related subject. The hospital has a thousand ears—and all of them will be listening to us." He looked at her sadly. "I'd better leave now."

"I'll say goodbye to the kids before I go." How could she sound so normal, Kate wondered, when her heart was being wrenched in two?

Sadly, silently, she went to find the children.

THE DAYS THAT FOLLOWED were endless.

"Gee, Katie, I wish you'd go with us. Tony would love to have you come," Molly cajoled.

"You know better than that. He didn't come here to visit you so he could have me tagging along. Anyway, there's nothing worse than being a third wheel."

"If you tell me enough times, I suppose I'll have to believe you," Molly said with exasperation. "It's just that I worry about you, and I haven't had much time to see you."

Kate smiled. Between work, Tony, Jerry and a stack of mail that would daunt a rock star, Molly was too deeply engrossed in her own love life to worry about Kate's.

"Run along, Molly. Tony's only here for a few days. You can talk to me anytime."

"Are you absolutely sure?" Molly frowned as she backed toward the door.

"Positive! Now leave before I have to chase you out with a broom!"

Kate sank wearily onto the smooth, cottony coolness of her sofa. Stretching out her bare legs to their full length, she lay staring at the ceiling.

Another quiet weekend in an unending string of them. These had been the longest four weeks of Kate's life. Since

Amy's legal actions had driven her and Chase apart, they'd said nothing more to each other than "good morning" and "good night." She'd hung onto the quick glimpses of him in the hospital corridors with the desperation of a drowning person, but there was never anything more—no flicker of an eyelid, no familiar twist of a lip, no physical signal that he was as lonely as she.

Kate flipped over onto her stomach and gave a loud sigh.

He had no choice, she supposed. He was fighting for his children. She'd missed Nathan and Emily these past weeks, too—it was difficult to imagine how their father might feel if he lost them completely.

"Anybody home?" A brisk rapping at the door distracted Kate from her thoughts.

"Sure. Just a minute." She swung off the couch and hurried to see who her visitor was.

"Marlis! Hi. How are you?"

"Fine. I was at that great bakery a couple of blocks away and I decided I'd stop by and see if you had a glass of iced tea for a weary shopper."

"You bet." Kate was delighted to see her friend, relieved that Marlis's arrival had rescued her from another moping session. "Peppermint tea all right?"

"Perfect."

Marlis settled herself on the couch as Kate filled two glasses.

"So, have you heard the latest?"

"Latest what?" Kate asked cautiously.

"The big malpractice suit. Somebody's suing the hospital." Marlis glanced craftily at Kate and added, "I hear Dr. Kincaid is very upset."

"Oh?" Kate hoped she sounded more casual than she felt.

"I've also heard the huge figures that the hospital pays in malpractice insurance already. Now that's going to skyrocket again. More budget problems for the hospital."

Another obstacle tossed into the path of Chase's dream. Then a chill rippled through Kate, one that left her cold even in the summer's heat.

If Chase didn't get the financing for the geriatric wing, and if he lost the children to Amy who still lived in Chicago, there would be no reason for him to stay in Fargo. None at all. He'd have to be near Nathan and Emily. His only choice would be to sell his house here and move back to Chicago. Perhaps he'd even buy a house in his old neighborhood. Kate grimaced as the next thought occurred to her. Perhaps he'd even start having meals with Amy and the children again.

"Are you all right?"

Kate opened her eyes to see Marlis staring straight into them.

"Fine." She brushed a hand across her forehead. "I guess I'm not too good in the heat."

"You should get a bigger air conditioner. That little thing is going to wear out just keeping it livable in here."

"Good idea," Kate agreed, her mind a million miles away from Marlis's small talk. "More tea?"

"No. I just wanted to put my feet up for a minute. Anyway, I'd better leave you alone to work."

"Work?" Kate asked blankly. "On what?"

"Facts. Figures. Whatever you're going to need for the negotiations."

Kate groaned. "Oh, that."

Why the board had decided to negotiate for salaries this month was beyond her. No doubt it had something to do with projecting a budget for the next calendar year, but Kate had a hunch that there was a hidden agenda, as well, probably connected with the financier who was waiting to decide to which hospital he would donate his geriatric wing.

"Actually, I hadn't thought too much about it."

Marlis's eyes widened. "But you're the head of the collective-bargaining unit. You're supposed to represent us!" Seeing the anguished look on Kate's face, she added, "Don't worry. You'll do just great. You haven't failed us yet, and you've had to face Kincaid before."

"Kincaid?" Kate asked weakly.

"Sure. Didn't you know? The board asked him to speak for them on the issue. It's going to be us and them on Monday night, Kate. You and the nurses versus Kincaid and the hospital board. Should be exciting."

Exciting? Kate thought as she closed the door behind her friend. Maybe. If you thought lynchings, executions and mutilations were exciting. She hadn't realized she and Chase—just the two of them—would be confronting each other over the nurses' salary issue. Then a wry smile twisted her lips. There was only one good thing she could see in all of this. It was an excuse to see Chase.

MONDAY EVENING approached too slowly, yet arrived too quickly.

Kate, in a severely tailored emerald dress that did nothing to hide her natural curves, was seated behind a large conference table, tapping her foot and wanting to be sick. The hospital board filed in, one at a time, all in dark suits and white shirts. For one wildly fanciful moment, Kate pictured herself attending a convention of penguins.

Several of the nurses who were off duty had already arrived. Marlis and Molly were in the back row, alternately giving Kate thumbs-up signs and worried glances.

At one minute to eight, Chase walked in.

He was thinner. As he bent to speak with the president of the hospital board she could see his belt gape away from his body and she noticed a little too much room in his shirt. Yet somehow, he'd become more attractive than ever this past month—if that were possible. His skin was a rich golden color, the deep lustrous color of old whiskey. As his skin had darkened, his hair had become blonder, no doubt because of time spent outdoors with the children and the new puppy.

Kate shuffled her feet beneath her desk. She'd lost a few pounds herself these past weeks. Food tasted like sawdust and she'd had no interest in cooking. On the days she'd forgotten to shop and there was no yogurt or cold cereal in the house, she hadn't eaten at all. Her hunger was for something far more complex than food.

"I believe we're about ready to begin," the board president announced. "There are several items on the agenda, but since we have so many observers here concerned with the nurses' salary issue, I believe we should begin with that. All right with you, Dr. Kincaid?"

"Just fine, sir." Chase glanced at Kate impassively.

"You may begin."

Chase shuffled the stack of papers he had before him as he rose. Then, rather than taking his papers with him, he slid his hands into the pockets of his suit and began to pace the room.

It was a good trick, Kate realized. It gave him the air of an injured storyteller about to impart a sad tale of insufficient finances and greedy nurses.

Her hunch was correct. Minutes into Chase's speech, even *she* was wondering how any of them dared ask for even a nickel more on their paychecks—especially when this big, benevolent hospital was doing so much for all of them. As she watched him pace and listened to the honeyed flow of his words, a new emotion began to flow through her. Stubbornness.

Chase Kincaid might be able to charm her straight out of her mind, but that didn't mean she was going to allow him to talk his way out of a pay raise for her and her colleagues. She hadn't learned to stand up to her rowdy, undisciplined brothers for nothing! Kate's jaw jutted out and she dug her heels into the spongy carpet of the conference-room floor. Whatever had gone on between her and Chase, whatever feelings she had, didn't count here. This was business—down and dirty!

"And so you see, ladies and gentlemen, taking into consideration increased competition, lowered occupancy rates, rising supply costs, rising plant costs, the looming specter of even larger insurance premiums, as well as all the other expenses I've outlined, the board simply does not feel it is feasible—or even possible—to offer a full cost-of-living raise at this time. We ask you, then, to give serious consideration to accepting a fraction of that figure." He cast a pleading little-boy look at the nurses, both male and female, in the audience, "If things turn around in twelve months, I guarantee your suggestions and requests will be given first priority—"

"I think we should be given first priority now."

Startled, Chase spun on his heel. Kate pushed back her chair and rose to her full height, head held high, chin forward, unaware of how her rigid, angry back pulled on the front of her dress, leaving a charming little gap at the neckline just below Chase's eye level.

"Ms Matthews?" He said her name with a breathiness that reminded Kate of their evening together in the park.

But she couldn't let the images in her mind hamper her.

"You've done a very eloquent job of explaining the importance of maintaining the hospital's facilities, Dr. Kincaid. And you've argued admirably about the importance of keeping full malpractice coverage. Indeed, you've almost made us feel sorry for the poor drug and supply manufacturers who are demanding twenty and thirty percent more for their products today than they did a year ago." She moved from behind the table to meet him face-to-face. More than anything she wanted to run her fingers through his hair and savor once again the taste and smell of him. Instead she kept her distance and continued.

"In fact, I'm sure that if we could afford it, most of the nurses in this room would love to volunteer their time to caring for their patients. But the fact is, none of us can afford to volunteer our time, yet that's virtually what you're asking us to do. You're asking us to work extra hours each day for free." She skewered him with her gaze. "We *deserve* those raises. This staff works hard and long."

"I'm hardly asking you to work for free...." He moved closer to her and Kate could feel the electricity his body generated in hers. It had been so long....

"No? Let's take a hypothetical situation." Kate walked briskly toward a portable blackboard in the corner of the room and dragged it to the center. She picked up a piece of chalk and began to write down her calculations. Her hands were trembling, Kate noticed with irritation.

"Say we're working eight-hour shifts and being paid ten dollars an hour. Perhaps the standard wage for our colleagues at another local hospital is being raised to fifteen dollars an hour. That means that, for an eight-hour shift, we earn eighty dollars. Correct?" Was that a smile hovering at the corners of his mouth?

"And our hypothetical colleagues' hypothetical checks come to one hundred and twenty dollars for the same amount of work." Kate scratched out the figures on the blackboard. He'd moved closer. She could smell the musky fragrance of his cologne.

"That means we have the choice of leaving our jobs and going to work at that other hospital, or giving up two to four hours of our salary to do volunteer nursing."

"Are you saying that, in such a situation all these nurses would quit if we didn't give them a pay raise?" a board member put in.

"Our qualified personnel would have no difficulty gaining employment elsewhere, Doctor. Are you willing to take that chance?"

A little gasp came from the nurses in the audience. Kate steeled herself. What she was doing was terribly risky, but that was one thing her brothers had done for her—taught her to play poker. Now she was calling the board's—and Chase's—bluff.

It worked.

"I hardly think it's necessary to go that far, Ms Matthews," Chase said. "Perhaps if you want to give us a more detailed outline of what your group would like to see."

The tension seeped out of Kate. "Certainly. I've photocopied some information..."

NOT UNTIL AFTER MIDNIGHT did the last of the board members and onlookers file from the conference room. Everyone looked exhausted, none more so than Chase and Kate.

"You were pretty wicked tonight," he said to her when they were alone in the hallway.

"Do you think it will do any good?"

He shrugged. "Frankly I don't know. I'm in a difficult position, knowing that if the budget doesn't come up black I'm not doing my job, yet seeing your side of things."

It was difficult for her, too, Kate mused. She'd had to choose between doing her job as negotiator and taking the risk of toppling the budget, which would mean seeing Chase lose his position as administrator and perhaps even move back to Chicago. Still, she'd committed herself to the responsibility of being the nurses' spokesperson. Chase wouldn't respect her, nor would she respect herself, for doing any less than her best.

"I was afraid I might explode tonight," he was saying. "Every time you leaned over to write on that darned blackboard—"

"Chase!" she hissed.

"There's no one here now. We've got a legitimate excuse for being together—for a few minutes, anyway."

She moved eagerly, willingly, into the arms he extended.

"Kate, oh Kate," he murmured, kissing her from the crown of her pale silken head, across her forehead, and down to her waiting lips.

His kiss was filled with a longing and a passion that Kate met with equal intensity. Finally Chase pulled back to gaze at her. He threaded his long surgeon's fingers through the tumble of fine hair that had fallen over her eyes.

"One more kiss and then I'd better go."

She nodded, her lips feeling full, warm, bruised, yet hungry for more. Kate raised herself onto her toes and leaned into him.

He lingered on her lips to take a final taste of her. Slowly, regretfully, he drew away. Then he turned and walked to the door. When he glanced back at her, his eyes were filled with anguish.

"Chase?" Kate said. "What about Amy? And the children?"

The look of pain deepened. "I don't know. I really don't know. Maybe this is goodbye, Kate."

He turned quickly without another word, and the door behind him slammed with a dreadful finality.

CHAPTER THIRTEEN

IT WAS OVER. Kate was certain. His final kiss had told her more eloquently than words. She could never ask him to choose between her and the children; Chase knew that and so did she. Kate stared out the window into the treetops. Over. Over. Over.

When the telephone rang, she reached lethargically for the receiver.

"Kate? Molly. Where are you?"

"Right here."

"No, I mean at work. Why haven't you been at work?"

"I decided to take a few days off. I'll be back on Monday."

"Oh. I thought maybe you were sick."

Not physically.

"I'm fine. Just a little tired. Too much negotiating, I guess."

"Is there any word on what the board decided about salaries?"

"Not that I've heard." There seemed to be a shroud of ominous silence surrounding the decision.

"Well, whatever they decide, the consensus is that you did a terrific job."

"Thanks."

"Are you sure you're all right? You sound funny."

"Really, I'm fine. I must have dozed off," Kate fibbed.

"Oh. Sorry I woke you. I'll let you go now. Call me soon."

Kate hung up the receiver with the same listlessness that she'd performed every other act in the past few days.

"Well, my friend," she said aloud to fill the emptiness, "you should do something constructive with your vacation. Clean cupboards, maybe. Or wash walls." She stared around her, hands on her hips. "But nothing around here ever gets dirty." She was home so little as a rule that nothing ever got out of place, and Melvin was hardly a messy animal. Her apartment was nearly as sterile as the hospital.

Everyone seemed to be conspiring to keep her and Chase apart—some faceless, nameless philanthropist who had the power to take his geriatric wing to any hospital in the country, the lawyers who warned that they must not see each other and, of course, Amy.

She curled onto the couch and wrapped her arms around her middle, trying to hug away the ache she felt inside. But it would not leave. Nothing could drive it away but having Chase in her arms. The ache would be there forever.

Kate was so engrossed in self-pity that she almost didn't answer the doorbell. Finally, after the seventh chime, she gave in. "I'm coming! Just wait!" She ran downstairs and opened the door.

"Were you in the shower?"

How could Chase stand there like that, looking as if he'd just dropped her off yesterday and was arriving today to finish their conversation? Kate stared at him stupidly, her mouth hanging open.

"Aren't you going to invite me in?"

"Yes. No. I don't know. Am I supposed to?"

"It's customary. Most people don't entertain on the front steps."

"But your lawyer said—"

"He's an old fuddy-duddy. A terrific lawyer, but an old fuddy-duddy."

"Are you sure?" Her mind was reeling with questions.

"Positive. But I have to run back to the car for a minute. I left some things in there just in case you weren't home."

"Okay, but..."

He was already gone. Kate stumbled backward into the house. What was going on? It was as if she'd been at a wake and then the deceased had cheerfully popped up from the casket. Before she could sort out her questions, he was back, this time with his arms full.

"Balloons?" Kate gasped. "And roses?"

"And champagne and chocolate-chip cookies. Did I get anything you like?"

"Yes. Everything. But why...?"

He turned a brilliant smile on her. "Amy's dropped her change-of-custody suit. We have to celebrate." Chase matter-of-factly marched upstairs, Kate behind him, walked into her apartment and placed his packages on the coffee table. The helium balloons—ten of them—floated to the ceiling.

"She dropped the suit?" Kate repeated, too stunned to take it all in. "Now?" Just when she'd convinced herself that Chase would never be truly free?

"You sound like an echo," Chase commented cheerfully. "Nathan and Emily are half mine again. Just like the biology." He grinned wickedly. "You do know how that happens, don't you?"

Kate ignored him. "Why? Why should she go to all this trouble and then just drop it like that? I thought she wanted full custody of the kids."

"So did she—until she had it."

"Huh?"

"I thought Amy needed to have her eyes opened. I sent the kids home to their mother for a while. Actually it was the first time she'd had to be with them through that many unbroken days of summer vacation since the divorce." He grinned. "An eleven- and a thirteen-year-old can be more of a handful than she remembered."

"What did they do?" Kate asked suspiciously. "They didn't pull any pranks, did they?"

Chase chuckled. "You know Nathan. He decided that the best way to solve the problem was to show his mother that having responsibility for two kids was just too much for one parent to handle—especially when there was another perfectly good parent waiting in the wings."

"I don't think I want to know about this," Kate murmured, dropping to the couch. "It smacks of writing love letters to strangers."

Chase nodded. "The kids weren't bad. It's just that Amy's found a new man, someone who doesn't have children—and doesn't really want a ready-made family. Apparently he didn't always understand when Mom was called home in the middle of a date."

"Or had to leave an embrace to chase away a nightmare."

"You've got the idea. Anyway, Amy has decided that she doesn't want to be quite so encumbered, so joint custody will be just fine, thank you. In fact, we're reversing schedules and the children will stay with me during the school year."

Kate clapped her hands in delight. "That means we can talk again?"

"Or do whatever we want." The words came from low in his throat and gave her an odd pulsing feeling in the pit of her stomach.

To distract herself, she opened the bag of chocolate-chip cookies and bit into one. "Yum. Fresh."

"Nothing but the best for you." As he moved closer she could smell the heady scent of his cologne. It was a struggle to keep her hands from burrowing into the front of his shirt.

Kate gave him a questioning glance.

"Which brings me to my next point."

"Which is?"

"Nurses' salaries."

Kate sat a little straighter.

"Against my better judgment, and at the risk of losing the funding for the geriatric wing, I went to bat for you nurses and your pay raise."

"Oh, Chase—"

He held up his hand. "Don't thank me. I know how invaluable good nurses are. I'm not about to treat them as second-class citizens in my hospital. Anyway, they're going to give your suggestions a trial run. If the new methods work, fine. If they don't, we go back to the old ways. You'll have twelve months to prove your ideas. In addition, they've agreed to a small salary increase—" he clamped his hand over Kate's mouth to keep her from interrupting "—and I'm hoping that once the nurses live up to the new trust and authority we're placing in them, negotiating another raise will be easy. The ball's in your court now, kiddo."

"But what about the financing for the geriatric wing?"

Chase shrugged. "The jury's still out on that one. I think we'll pull in pretty close to budget." A grin quirked at the corner of his mouth. "I did hear via the grapevine that our philanthropist has recently spent a good deal of time in hospitals and has a special fondness and gratitude for some of the nurses who cared for him. Maybe if we're only a little over budget, we can tell him why—because we want to recognize our nurses as the professionals they are."

Kate fell back against the cushions of the couch. "I can't believe it! I simply can't believe it!"

Chase sprawled on the couch beside her and crossed his legs. "Believe it. Do you have any glasses? I want to get into this champagne."

Dazedly Kate rose to go into her small kitchen. Then, taking two fluted champagne glasses—the only two she owned—from the china cabinet, she passed them to Chase. He deftly uncorked the bottle and poured the glistening liquid.

"Good," he proclaimed. "Now taste." He handed her a glass. As she sipped her champagne, the frothy little bubbles flew up her nose. Kate giggled.

"Now dip a chocolate-chip cookie in it."

"Ugh."

"You'd be surprised. Here, share mine." He slipped a cookie between his teeth and offered it to her.

It was an offer she couldn't refuse. As she nibbled at her half of the cookie, she was sidetracked by a delectable pair of masculine lips. When she was so breathless she thought she'd faint, Kate drew away to ask, "What about the champagne?"

Chase, his eyes hooded and smoky, muttered, "What about it?" and gently pushed her into a reclining position on the couch. His weight on her was a wonderful heaviness. His hands coasted over her, exploring, touching. Kate's head dropped back in sheer bliss. Chase found the gentle curve of her neck, that little hollow in the center of her collarbone, and dipped his tongue into it. Kate tensed with pleasure.

His lips lingered there, revelling in her smoothness. Kate's arms tightened around his neck and held him fast. Then reason came creeping back to her, one unwelcome bit at a time.

"Chase?"

"Hmm?" His tongue was caressing her ear, sending shudders of pleasure down her spine.

Kate squirmed a little, moving him off her slightly. There was more to be settled before she could give herself fully to this splendid activity. "What about us?"

"What about us?" He frowned and sat up, raking his fingers through his hair, his breath still ragged. "Surely you can figure it out!"

Kate swallowed. "Don't be angry. It's just that . . ." Her voice trailed away and she smiled weakly. "Well, I guess I just need to know."

Instead of answering her, he changed the subject.

"Kate, who painted that portrait of me and the children that they gave me for my birthday?"

Stunned by this odd twist in their conversation, she said, "Hank Burns. He works at the hospital. Is something wrong? Don't you like it?"

Chase shook his head somberly. "No, not really—"

"The children saved all their money for months for that portrait!" Kate gasped, irate as a mother hen. "What's wrong with it?"

"I'm afraid something's missing."

"Missing?" Kate's face was blank. "What's missing?"

Chase's eyes gleamed, and the amber flecks danced in the fading afternoon light. "You."

"Me?" she squeaked.

Chase nodded. "You're what's missing. Will you marry me, Kate? I want you in my family portrait from now on."

"Me?" she repeated.

He chuckled and cradled her face in his hands. "You wanted to know, Kate. And now you do. I've never loved anyone more than I love you."

"But Amy—"

"You and Amy are different women, Kate. You're in a class all by yourself. Believe that."

She traced a fingertip along the line of his jaw, as a bubble of happiness welled up inside her. "Do you know what I love most about you, Chase? Your honesty. You've never lied to me before and I don't think you're lying now."

The somberness in his eyes changed to a twinkle. "You love that best? My honesty? What about my body?"

Kate laughed aloud at the sudden, comical switch in his demeanor. She studied him theatrically, head to one side. "Your body? It's rather a nice specimen." She squinted intently at the trim line of his torso as it disappeared into the waistband of his trousers. "In fact, I've had a purely clinical interest in your body for some time now."

"You have?" Chase said with obvious delight. "What a coincidence! I've felt the same way about yours!" His grin turned wicked. "In fact, I can tell you the day and hour at which my, ahem, fascination, started."

"Really?" Kate parried. "How is that possible?"

"I asked that very question the first time I saw you sunbathing outside your house." He tipped his head back and gazed at the ceiling. " 'How is that possible?' I said to myself. 'How can that scrap of a bathing suit contain that lush body?' " He glanced at her playfully. "Actually I was hoping the fabric would give way, but no such luck."

Before she could respond, he stood up and drew Kate to her feet, holding her gently away from him as he asked, "Well, will you? Marry me? Be in my family picture? Forever?"

"Yes. Yes!" Laughing, crying, glowing, Kate fell into his arms.

Forever.

It hardly seemed long enough.

EPILOGUE

KATE TIPTOED across the bedroom so as not to wake Nathan and Emily—or the dog—and dropped the sheer froth of her negligée to the floor. It was two in the morning.

Chase was sprawled across the bed, still in his shirt and trousers, the article he was writing on specialization in geriatric medicine scattered over the spread.

Silently Kate collected the papers. Her husband was going to be a household word in the ranks of physicians one day soon. It was already beginning to happen with the addition of the geriatric wing at St. Mike's. Kate glanced over the pages. He'd poured his heart and soul into this one. Then she noticed the small folded note on her pillow. She swept the other papers to the bedside stand and curled onto the corner of the bed to read:

Dear KIM,
I am a doctor and I live in Fargo, North Dakota. I'm newly married. I love my wife very much, but she's working the evening shift all week long, so I've hardly had a chance to speak to her. I've been thinking that it's time to add a baby to our family. What do you think?

Please let me know by leaving a note under my pillow. I'll be waiting to hear from you.

Sincerely,
C.G.

Smiling broadly, Kate slipped the straps of her nightgown from her shoulders and allowed it to fall to the floor.

Carefully she moved her hand beneath Chase's pillow and wiggled her fingers. He was awake in a moment, his eyes wide and clear.

"I have a message from your pen pal," she began huskily.

"Oh?" Kate caught a glimmer of his smile as he leaned toward the bedside stand and switched off the light. "What did she say?" The question came out of the darkness.

"A definite, unqualified yes."

"We're in agreement then?" His hand slid around her shoulders.

"Without a doubt," Kate managed, as his lips came down on hers in a warm and passionate kiss. "How lucky for me."

His soft laugh floated through the darkness. "For both of us, Kate. For both of us."

INDULGE A LITTLE SWEEPSTAKES

OFFICIAL RULES

SWEEPSTAKES RULES AND REGULATIONS. NO PURCHASE NECESSARY.

1. NO PURCHASE NECESSARY. To enter complete the official entry form and return with the invoice in the envelope provided. Or you may enter by printing your name, complete address and your daytime phone number on a 3 x 5 piece of paper. Include with your entry the hand printed words "Indulge A Little Sweepstakes." Mail your entry to: Indulge A Little Sweepstakes, P.O. Box 1397, Buffalo, NY 14269-1397. No mechanically reproduced entries accepted. Not responsible for late, lost, misdirected mail, or printing errors.

2. Three winners, one per month (Sept. 30, 1989, October 31, 1989 and November 30, 1989), will be selected in random drawings. All entries received prior to the drawing date will be eligible for that month's prize. This sweepstakes is under the supervision of MARDEN-KANE, INC. an independent judging organization whose decisions are final and binding. Winners will be notified by telephone and may be required to execute an affidavit of eligibility and release which must be returned within 14 days, or an alternate winner will be selected.

3. Prizes: 1st Grand Prize (1) a trip for two to Disneyworld in Orlando, Florida. Trip includes round trip air transportation, hotel accommodations for seven days and six nights, plus up to $700 expense money (ARV $3,500). 2nd Grand Prize (1) a seven-night Chandris Caribbean Cruise for two includes transportation from nearest major airport, accommodations, meals plus up to $1,000 in expense money (ARV $4,300). 3rd Grand Prize (1) a ten day Hawaiian holiday for two includes round trip air transportation for two, hotel accommodations, sightseeing, plus up to $1,200 in spending money (ARV $7,700). All trips subject to availability and must be taken as outlined on the entry form.

4. Sweepstakes open to residents of the U.S. and Canada 18 years or older except employees and the families of Torstar Corp., its affiliates, subsidiaries and Marden-Kane, Inc. and all other agencies and persons connected with conducting this sweepstakes. All Federal, State and local laws and regulations apply. Void wherever prohibited or restricted by law. Taxes, if any are the sole responsibility of the prize winners. Canadian winners will be required to answer a skill testing question. Winners consent to the use of their name, photograph and/or likeness for publicity purposes without additional compensation.

5. For a list of prize winners, send a stamped, self-addressed envelope to Indulge A Little Sweepstakes Winners, P.O. Box 701, Sayreville, NJ 08871.

 DL-SWPS

INDULGE A LITTLE SWEEPSTAKES

OFFICIAL RULES

SWEEPSTAKES RULES AND REGULATIONS. NO PURCHASE NECESSARY.

1. NO PURCHASE NECESSARY. To enter complete the official entry form and return with the invoice in the envelope provided. Or you may enter by printing your name, complete address and your daytime phone number on a 3 x 5 piece of paper. Include with your entry the hand printed words "Indulge A Little Sweepstakes." Mail your entry to: Indulge A Little Sweepstakes, P.O. Box 1397, Buffalo, NY 14269-1397. No mechanically reproduced entries accepted. Not responsible for late, lost, misdirected mail, or printing errors.

2. Three winners, one per month (Sept. 30, 1989, October 31, 1989 and November 30, 1989), will be selected in random drawings. All entries received prior to the drawing date will be eligible for that month's prize. This sweepstakes is under the supervision of MARDEN-KANE, INC. an independent judging organization whose decisions are final and binding. Winners will be notified by telephone and may be required to execute an affidavit of eligibility and release which must be returned within 14 days, or an alternate winner will be selected.

3. Prizes: 1st Grand Prize (1) a trip for two to Disneyworld in Orlando, Florida. Trip includes round trip air transportation, hotel accommodations for seven days and six nights, plus up to $700 expense money (ARV $3,500). 2nd Grand Prize (1) a seven-night Chandris Caribbean Cruise for two includes transportation from nearest major airport, accommodations, meals plus up to $1,000 in expense money (ARV $4,300). 3rd Grand Prize (1) a ten-day Hawaiian holiday for two includes round trip air transportation for two, hotel accommodations, sightseeing, plus up to $1,200 in spending money (ARV $7,700). All trips subject to availability and must be taken as outlined on the entry form.

4. Sweepstakes open to residents of the U.S. and Canada 18 years or older except employees and the families of Torstar Corp., its affiliates, subsidiaries and Marden-Kane, Inc. and all other agencies and persons connected with conducting this sweepstakes. All Federal, State and local laws and regulations apply. Void wherever prohibited or restricted by law. Taxes, if any are the sole responsibility of the prize winners. Canadian winners will be required to answer a skill testing question. Winners consent to the use of their name, photograph and/or likeness for publicity purposes without additional compensation.

5. For a list of prize winners, send a stamped, self-addressed envelope to Indulge A Little Sweepstakes Winners, P.O. Box 701, Sayreville, NJ 08871.

© 1989 HARLEQUIN ENTERPRISES LTD. DL-SWPS

INDULGE A LITTLE—WIN A LOT!

Summer of '89 Subscribers-Only Sweepstakes

OFFICIAL ENTRY FORM

This entry must be received by: Nov. 30, 1989
This month's winner will be notified by: Dec. 7, 1989
Trip must be taken between: Jan. 7, 1990–Jan. 7, 1991

YES, I want to win the 3-Island Hawaiian vacation for two! I understand the prize includes round-trip airfare, first-class hotels, and a daily allowance as revealed on the "Wallet" scratch-off card.

Name____________________________

Address____________________________

City__________ State/Prov.______ Zip/Postal Code______

Daytime phone number____________________
Area code

Return entries with invoice in envelope provided. Each book in this shipment has two entry coupons—and the more coupons you enter, the better your chances of winning!

DINDL-3

INDULGE A LITTLE—WIN A LOT!

Summer of '89 Subscribers-Only Sweepstakes

OFFICIAL ENTRY FORM

This entry must be received by: Nov. 30, 1989
This month's winner will be notified by: Dec. 7, 1989
Trip must be taken between: Jan. 7, 1990–Jan. 7, 1991

YES, I want to win the 3-Island Hawaiian vacation for two! I understand the prize includes round-trip airfare, first-class hotels, and a daily allowance as revealed on the "Wallet" scratch-off card.

Name____________________________

Address____________________________

City__________ State/Prov.______ Zip/Postal Code______

Daytime phone number____________________
Area code

Return entries with invoice in envelope provided. Each book in this shipment has two entry coupons—and the more coupons you enter, the better your chances of winning!

© 1989 HARLEQUIN ENTERPRISES LTD.

DINDL-3